LIQ-TROCITY

BY CHERAEE C.

By: Cheraee C.

LIQ-TROCITY

MOCY PUBLISHING
WWW.MOCYPUBLISHING.COM

Detroit, Michigan

Liq-Trocity

ISBN 978-1-940831-05-3
Copyright © 2014 by Cheraee C.

Published by Mocy Publishing, LLC.
Website: www.mocypublishing.com
Email: info@mocypublishing.com
Phone: (872) 216-6629

When shit got real...

"My brain is hanging upside down," was the daily aftermath of Chisel Simmons after his coast-to- coast pro basketball career became obsolete. No matter what he did to guarantee his success, his focus was remotely off, and he couldn't think logically without being easily side-tracked.

Chisel was a proficient, 10-year-Euroleague power forward who wore his number 7 jersey pompously. Everything changed when his physical aptitude shifted from athletic to un-athletic in a matter of seconds ending a fourth quarter.

Playing basketball overseas was the most optimistic decision that Chisel ever made for his basketball profession and everything was smooth at first, but life always finds an unyielding way to intervene. Oversea basketball players got paid less then what U.S. basketball players did, but they were spoiled with lots of amenities. They were given houses, cars, women, endorsements, clothing, more women, and anything they could ever envision. Chisel didn't have to spend a dime of his earnings, because he was worshipped by the sport, and the sport provided him with an affluent lifestyle he couldn't decline.

Just as Chisel was bypassing opponents, dribbling and crossing through the frontcourt, and scored the winning shot in his championship game; a game where his team excelled with a 111-78 blowout, something below his waist popped. Something felt looser than it ever felt before. Chisel's body buckled down on the court and the basketball went rolling to the stands. Chisel was in excruciating pain when paramedics were called to his aching rescue. After numerous imaging tests, an MRI, and annoying ass doctors, Chisel found out that he tore his ACL (anterior cruciate ligament) which was both a common and uncommon injury for a typical basketball star.

After being told that he would never be able to play basketball again on so many rehab and surgical occasions, Chisel knew damn well his career was over and preferred to embark on another career pathway because there was no way in hell he was going to risk injuring himself so traumatically again. Surgeries, rehabs, and doctors just weren't his thing, not to mention all the pain that he had to endure suffering, recuperating, and healing from his injury was unforgettable. Using crunches, limited physical activity, and wearing a leg brace wasn't his style either so Chisel began to self-medicate himself with alcohol. This loathsome period in his life became the beginning of a habit and future habits that he was never going to be able to shake out of his re-structured system.

Chisel's liquid demons made him become verbally abusive towards women, insecure, paranoid, sleep deprived, develop trust issues, act very irrationally and idiotically in the public eye, unsympathetic, and feel invalid. His liquid demons pretty much turned him into an unrecognizable monster at intoxicating levels.

Chisel had a house so grandiose that it should've been featured on MTV Crib's for all of its perks and was just all-around grandeur. Chisel was a definite father of two sons, and two possible daughters. He was a ladies' man who changed women like he changed draws, with a wife still hanging on the back-burner. One day he planned to divorce his first and current wife, Haze Hilton, when he felt like Fed-Exing her ass back to Korea. Until then, he was just going to have to deal with her wifely bullshit, but since they   parated, and she was a hooker, her wifely bullshit was only going to get worst.

Years later, Chisel's money flow was like a car dealership full of armored money trucks loaded with stacks and racks of money. Chisel could do whatever the hell he wanted to do in his liquid life and nobody could stop him. From time to time, Chisel still made money off of his retired talent by doing interviews, hosting basketball events, hosting parties, private appearances, endorsements, and etc so he was never money-hungry.

The sad part about Chisel and his love life was that he put too much emphasis in color complexity in correlation with the women he chose to be with. He had a light skin and white skins is the right skin complex so he never found himself dating, fucking, or even eye-fucking a caramel skinned or dark skinned woman because his skin x was high and mighty. Chisel was definitely selling himself short, but as far as Chisel knew he knew everything, his preference was his preference, and nobody could tell him any different.

The light skinned and white skinned women he loved really loved him. They were never in love with him for the money, but he was too lost in addiction to grasp the true concept of love so he let his liquid dependence drive his women insane. As far as he was concerned no woman would ever be able to make him conquer his liquid fetishes not even his wife, not his daughter if and when he had one that wasn't in question, not a trick, not a side-bitch, and not even his own mother. Chisel was going to be an alcoholic until he drunk himself into a coma and died unless life decided differently.

In the meantime in between time Chisel had better get his shattered life together before his life was like paper shreds in a paper shredder because Chisel was going to have a rude awakening and it wasn't going to be

enough fire extinguishers to save his life from

burning into flames.

Table of Contents

Chapter 1: Drunken Love........................13

Chapter 2: Burn Baby Burn....................31

Chapter 3: A Day in Pandora's Box........42

Chapter 4: Deal or No Deal....................51

Chapter 5: Bull-Headed Mistress..............63

Chapter 6: Moaning Off The Hinges........82

Chapter 7: From Ashes To Dust..............96

Chapter 8: You Turning Me Off..............108

Chapter 9: The Bitch Confesses..............122

Chapter 10: Angel Eyes...........................136

Chapter 11: Rebellious Craves.................158

Chapter 12: Pain or Pleasure....................177

Chapter 13: Nose Candy...........................188

Chapter 14: Off The Wall.........................206

Chapter 15: Sleeping with The Enemy.....217

Chapter 16: Comatose..............................231

Chapter 1: Drunken Love

A double-shot takes the pain away…

Gigantic, black, massive, smoke balls and orangish-yellow flames galloped and mounted through the humid air. Walls, stairs, rooms, and floors were vanquishing by the minute like objects do in the midst of urban fog. Neighbors were still bed bound by their tiresome so nobody had a clue, a nose-filling clue, or an eye-latching clue of what was diminishing beside them. Still the scene was siren free, unexpected, and undetected. Meteorologists couldn't even measure the wind velocity because it wasn't one to quantum.

Arson was like an hourly epidemic spreading across the U.S. edges and curves where law breakers, convicts, rivals, rebels and etc displayed the willful or malicious burning of private property of a building, vehicle, or a home with criminal or fraudulent intent. In today's society the younger generations lacked environmental respect, had an anger-raging poise, and dared to test their fate.

Detroit was a very scorched metropolis and so were all the outlying cities surrounding it. Chisel was laid back in his driver seat between his backseat and his car rooftop. He was all alone on the bull's-eye of Detroit's eastside in his CTS Cadillac like sleeping in your car was the most economical way to save money. Trying to accumulate some body heat, Chisel kept his Al Wissam coat zipped up from waist to neck. Still half tipsy from yesterday's liquid love, Chisel couldn't remember all of the events that transpired in his alcoholic life. His trunk was loaded, stacked, and packed with some of his most valuable belongings because he knew he had screwed up big somehow he just didn't remember exactly how.

"Look you bum ass dumb ass slime ball!" Haze poked her index finger at Chisel's chest scowling dead in his yellowish-reddish eyes.

"This is my fucking house and I want your drunken ass out! Since you don't want to quit drinking stay the fuck away from me and your son!"

"Bitch you got me confused when did this become your house? You better take your watermelon head ass home!"

"Motherfucker won't you just go! You ain't shit and you ain't never going to be shit with your short dick ass!" (Trigger) Chisel had a hundred triggers that could set him off like the speed of light at any given time. And saying he wasn't shit, and wasn't never to going to be shit was one speedy way to do it. Growing up Chisel's mother always scarred him with those same blurred lines which left him with strong disregards towards women. In his menacing eyes every woman was just like his mother; she was automatically a liar, a conniver, and a cheater sums it all up with or without proof.

Never try to stroke a man's ego when he is already liable to cause bodily harm to you just on the strength of your gender. Haze was definitely going to learn today.

"Bitch you better watch how you talk to me in my house!" Immediately Chisel headed for Haze in a Jason crazed kind of walk and slung her out of her house shoes like a plastic bag in the wind.

"Or what? What you gonna do? What is your bottle-schizoid self gonna do to me that hasn't already been done? I can't even count on my fingers and toes how many times we have went through this same shit!"

Haze was kicking her legs forcefully like a toddler throwing a tantrum screaming hoarsely, "let me go! Let me go!"

"I'm not letting you go I'm about to give you this dick. Since this dick is so little let's see if you can take it right here, right now." Chisel smacked Haze's back on his dining room table and began yanking down her leggings.

"Chisel stop! I hate you! Leave me alone! Just go before I call the police on you!" Haze began crying and struggling with her drunken husband.

"I hate you too, but you bout to take this dick."

Chisel had Haze's leggings down to her ashy ankles when Chisel Jr. woke up from his nap and came into the room. Chisel seeing his son snapped him out of his drunken rampage and made him realize that he was about to make a string of mistakes so he decided the best thing for him to do was to eliminate himself from the premises. Before leaving Chisel went in his bedroom and snatched up as many of his things as he possibly could and filled them up in his car. He figured it was best for him to stay away from his house for a week or so that he could sober up.

The more and more Chisel reflected on his legal migraine of a marriage, and the multiple reasons why he ended up astray in his luxurious car on a Saturday night, the more aggravated he became. Maybe if Chisel didn't have his stupid light bright pigmentation guidelines to dating he wouldn't always end up with the low-grade quality of women that he always ended up with. You can't pinpoint a physical description to a good woman even if it includes all the physical traits you desire. God sends you who he sends you and there is no defying his will.

Since Chisel was just a couple miles away from his best friend's Gregory's house, he figured he would pump up his CTS, hope for a nice, hot shower, and talk to Greg about his situation, but first he had to make a slight detour to the nearest liquor store and buy him a brew and a double shot of Extra Smooth. When

Chisel pulled up to Greg's place he noticed there was another vehicle hogging up his long, narrow driveway.

Damn Rosario is here. Why does this bitch have to be here every time I pop up over here to chill with my homeboy? I'm not trying to sound like a hater, but damn that bitch could stay at her own damn house sometimes. I just got finished arguing with my half of a bitch the last thing I want to do is argue with his bitch too. Typical women shit; she probably knew I was coming over here, and came over here just so she could start some shit with me. I really do think she gets a kick out of that shit. Rosario made Chisel real irritated because her and Chisel were always at each other's throats. No matter what holiday it was you couldn't leave them two alone together in a room not even if it was the green room on the Maury Show. Picture a boxing ring and Mayweather vs. Tyson throwing blows because that was the ideal Rosario vs. Chisel whenever they crossed paths.

Rosario and Gregory had been kicking it for like 8 months now and their relationship was just like any other relationship she had ever been in where the man never wants to sacrifice shit not even the last piece of a biscuit. Rosario wanted Gregory to get rid of all of his buster ass friends, because she wanted her man to only surround himself with productivity, and there was nothing charismatic about drinking, smoking, fighting, clubbing, or scamming. As far as she was concerned all they needed was each other anyway.

Chisel's phone had been on off mode

just so he wouldn't have to deal with none of his women's nonsense, but since he had to call Greg and let him know he was outside, he powered his phone on.

"Ring, Ring."

"What's shaking bro," Greg greeted in a jovial voice like he just got some morning play from his bedside vixen.

"I'm outside bro let me in."

"Cool I'll be at the side door in one second."

Once Greg let Chisel in the house, they went straight to the basement to Greg's man cave.

"You smell a little tart bro like funk and liquor what's going on?" Greg questioned Chisel who was lugging his best friend Milwaukee in his hand."

22

"And you smell like a combination of dick and pussy, but were not going to talk about smells. All I know is me and Haze got into a big fight last night and I woke up in my car this morning. And now here I am. I blacked out man. I really don't remember shit that happened during the argument."

"You really need to squash that bitch bro because I'm tired of y'all arguing. I know you need to slow down with the drinking, but she not all innocent neither. How can you respect a fucking hooker? I don't know why bitches think just because they have a baby they own a nigga and everything he owns is hers too."

"I'm tired of that bitch too bro, I don't know what my next move is going to be, but I know I need a shower, and I got some of my things in the car. Would it be cool if I left them here until I get myself together?"

"My home is your home, you know that shit is cool with me so go bring your shit in the house and get your funky ass in the shower. You know where everything at. I'm about to watch me an episode of First 48 right quick."

Chisel went outside, got all of his things out of his car, and put them in one of Greg's guest rooms. After he scrambled through his things and found him some fresh gear for the day, he gathered all of his male hygiene essentials and grabbed a towel and a washcloth out of the linen closet. Then he went into the bathroom, closed the door behind him, and turned on the shower. He continued to sip on his best friend Milwaukee while he waited on steady hot water still trying to remember how his future ex-wife and him got into it.

Rosario was still lying naked in Greg's bed daydreaming about their authentic love-making. She was wondering why he left her gentle grasp and still hadn't come back upstairs yet to rejoin her. Deciding she would go on the quest for her man, she put on her short, little, tight robe and proceeded downstairs. As Rosario's foot touched the last carpeted step and heard the shower running rapid, she figured Greg was in the bathroom taking a shower, and she wanted to join him. *Greg is so sweet I'm sure he's been waiting patiently in the shower for me to join him so we can finish where we left-off.* Rosario opened the bathroom door silently, and closed it back. She slipped off her bath robe and didn't understand why she saw clothes on the bathroom floor when all Greg had on was some basketball shorts. Since she thought that her and Greg were the only ones in the house, she opened the shower door and got the most nauseating shock of her life.

"Chisel what the fuck are you doing here!" Rosario was infuriated and lavished at the same time as she got a little peek at Chisel's rapturous physique. Gregory had never ever let any of his friends shower at his house, so Rosario couldn't understand what the hell made Chisel so special. Best friend or not she thought the shower was off limits.

"What you staring at? You want to join me or something!" Chisel was alarmed by Rosario's nakedness, but was intrigued with her enthralling body, but the last thing he wanted Greg to think was that he was trying to

26

fuck his woman.

"Negro please, I'm going to kill Greg!" Rosario made an ugly face at the thought of her doing something with Chisel and screamed as she hurried up and fastened her robe back on as tightly as she could. Once again, she went off on a Greg man hunt, and this time she was going to make sure the man she found was Greg himself.

"Greg where are you I'm about to beat the fuck out of you now!" Greg heard Rosario's screeches through his surround sound so he stormed up the basement stairs trying to figure out what he did this time.

"What's wrong baby what did I do now?"

"Why the fuck didn't you tell me Chisel was here? I just walked into the bathroom

27

naked as hell thinking that it was you in the shower about to hop right in with you. Are you fucking remedial or something?"

"I'm sorry babe for not telling you, but Chisel needed a shower bad as hell. I thought you were upstairs sleeping."

"Sorry doesn't cut it. Either he's going to leave or I'm going to leave, but I'm not about to deal with his drunken bullshit today. I told you I don't want him around me so what part of that didn't you understand?"

"Technically he wasn't around you, you came around him," Greg laughed and smiled with a big Joker smile.

"I'm not joking Greg."

"If you don't take your evil ass upstairs, I'm going to pinch your booty. He's going to be leaving shortly so chill."

"If he isn't gone in an hour I will be so you better choose wisely because the clock is ticking. We talk about this bullshit all the damn time. And whenever it comes down to the shit you never stick to your guns."   "Take your ass upstairs damn. I promise you I'll be up there in a minute," Greg directed in a playful manner.

When Chisel got out of the shower, he made sure the coast was actually clear. He went to the guest room where his things were, threw on his clothes, and got the hell up out of dodge. He didn't even bother to tell Greg he was leaving because clearly his little short stay was enough to cause havoc at his friend's place and that was the last thing he wanted to do. That's exactly why Rosario was a bitch and Chisel hated being around her. No matter what was going on she always had to put in her two cents like she lived with Greg and was always making Greg choose sides. *Ain't no sides bitch you know how the saying goes; bitches come and go, but friends are forever.*

Chisel never stayed anywhere long anyway; not even in his own house without having to relocate, and be at war with his alcoholic super-ego and his sober ID.

■■■■■■■■■■■■■■■■■■■■■■■■■■■■■■■■■■■■■■

Chapter 2: Burn, Baby, Burn

My broken heart is on fire....

The public liaison Sway Carter and his firefighter squad were fighting the tall and high flames at a miscellaneous house in a suburban neighborhood. It was 6:30 in the wee hours of the morning when the firefighters arrived on the site. It took two long, hot hours to finally spray the massive fire to rest.

Mr. Carter controlled and organized his team accordingly.

"More water power, more water power! Let's go! We don't have all day! Let's put this fire out now team! Y'all didn't graduate to become firefighters to babysit no fucking fire! You son of bitches are acting like amateurs! If y'all don't hurry up and contain this shit the whole neighborhood is going to be burnt down!"

When Mr. Carter accessed the scene, the team concluded that there wasn't any signs of life and the fire was ruled an arson. Firefighters were also going off a 911 call that they received from a young lady who claimed to be a neighborhood resident. The young lady reported the fire and made sure she let 911 dispatchers know that the homeowners were out of town and she saw the perpetrators fire-bomb the house on her way in from work. So firefighters went with what they knew, shut the fire down, and got the hell on ready to let the Clinton Township Police Department do their job.

***

Just as Chisel slammed his driver door shut and turned the key to revive his HEMI ignition, his phone began to vibrate uncontrollably like a two-way pager. Chisel really wasn't in the mood for talking, so he automatically answered his phone with an attitude.

"Hello."

"Yes can I please speak with Chisel Simmons?" A white female secretarial voice questioned.

"So who the fuck is this?"

"Do you live on the 4000 block of Rivergate Drive in Clinton Township, Michigan?"

"Yes I do can you please tell me what the fuck is going on?"

"There is no need to curse sir; authorities have a report....."

"Authorities have a report of what?"

"I'm calling from the Charter
Township of the Clinton Fire Department
because there has been a fire reported at your
residence that approximately started around
5:33 A.M."

"There must be some kind of mistake. I
haven't even been at my house so how could it
have caught on fire?"

"I know this might be upsetting and
hard to believe, but there was a fire. Luckily,
firefighters finally put the fire out about an
hour ago. The fire department has been trying
to reach you, but we kept getting your
voicemail. One of your neighbors gave us your
cellular number so we could contact you. I
don't think it was anyone in your house, but
you are going to have to file a report about this
matter as soon as possible."

Chisel wanted to think this bitch was bluffing, but who was he to call bluff when he bluffed all the time, 24/7, 7 days a week, 365 days a year. Only way to find out the truth was to go inspect his house himself.

"Something is not right about this. Y'all didn't put no fire out at my house, but thank you for the forewarning bye." Chisel hung right up in the girl's ears, but now he saw an importance to check up on his home sweet home so he hit the next ramp to East 94.

The ruins of Chisel's house weren't hard to magnify out the corners of his crooked eyes. The closer he got down his narrow block, the more his corneas trembled in his eye pockets. Five houses down, four houses down, three houses down, two houses down, his house. His 2,400 square foot brick domain was now physically dwindled from something to nothing. As he parked directly across from his use to be house, he stared at what was now just 2 acres of black, barren terrain. When Chisel glared north of him, he noticed he had a present waiting in front of him which was somebody in a gray foreign car. Somebody who shouldn't have been anywhere near this house after what she done. Somebody who should've just rode by and kept it pushing, but she had to check on the prognosis of her latest business deal.

Some men never ever showed emotion, and others just showed it very seldom, but Chisel was taking his fire very lightly as if it was thoroughly planned. He just lost everything I mean everything and didn't even bother to shed one single tear or one weep. He just lost the most expensive house he had ever

36

purchased in all of his homeowner years and he was still functioning normally. He just lost everything and it was taking everything in his power for him not to indulge on his liquid ecstasy. Instead he decided to step out of his car and take some of his steam off on his biggest problem in the universe which was his wife "Haze" so Chisel strolled up to his wife's car-side.

"Shouldn't you be out sucking and fucking or did you decide to substitute your dirtbag ways to set my house on fire?" Chisel teased Haze after she winded her slutty window down. Stunned at how quick he was to blame her; it wasn't like he was a one-woman man and at least she got paid to fuck. Chisel probably had a whole list of names he should've been blaming for his unfortunate loss. He should've written all of those names down, put them in a black magic hat, shook them up, and pulled a name out. Surely the lucky name he pulled out wasn't going to be Haze's.

Haze Hilton was a lustrous mixture of Korean and Black with 18-inch cognac colored hair, Taraji Henson eyebrows, glossy vanilla skin, and a video vixen booty you could sit a Heineken bottle on and it wouldn't fall. She had Victoria Secret breasts, and some Jai'Laye lips. She was 28 years young and was borderline Libra and Scorpio. Most Korean women were skinny and anorexic, but Haze was thick and pleasantly plumped. Men just never seemed to get with her program, despite her undeniable beauty and crudity.

"Come on baby, I know you don't think

I did this to us. You are my husband and that is something that I will cherish for the rest of my life. This was still my house no matter what our relationship status is. We had so many memories here. Why would I burn it down? Chisel Jr. and I were just there yesterday. Why would I do that?"

"Bitch please why won't you put me out my misery and divorce me already instead of continuing to make my life a living hell? I'm not going to stop calling you a bitch and I'm not going to change my ways for you or anybody else. I'm not going to stop telling you to eat a dick or kill yourself and I'm not going to stop drinking. So you can do whatever you want to do to me, but maybe if you give me a divorce I will be a lot nicer to you."

"You know what, I hope you freeze to

39

death while you gulping down that shot of vodka in your coat. I got better things to do then check up on your pathetic ass. You the one without a house not me so yeah why should I give a shit about your problems. If your phone wasn't always going to voicemail you would've got the memo. Now get the fuck away from my car and fix your house!" Haze shouted all fired up as she winded her window back up and moved her long Korean hair out her face so she could make her dirty money.

Chisel should've known she was going to use that lie, but if the fire happened today how come Haze couldn't get a hold of him? He turned his phone on. Why was she just sitting there staring at his house like it was a piece of meat instead of calling him? And why didn't she leave a message? She left a message any

40

other time. Maybe because she was GUILTY until proven innocent, but whatever the case was Chisel wiped the air to clear out the lung-clogging house debris and exhaust smoke that was congesting up his nostrils, hopped back in his car, and sped off until he couldn't speed off anymore.

∎∎∎∎∎∎∎∎∎∎∎∎∎∎∎∎∎∎∎∎∎∎∎∎∎∎∎∎∎∎∎∎∎∎∎∎∎ı

Chapter 3: A Day in Pandora's Box

Ain't no shame in my game....

34-year-old Chisel Simmons was absolutely gorgeous with more sex appeal then a Hollywood star. He was tall, light skinned, and so strikingly handsome that mirrors were even jealous of him. His goatee stayed razor-sharp in one unison connecting from his beard to his chin hairs to his sideburns. His only two known quirks was his womanizing tendencies and his hindering addiction of alcohol. At least those were the only two flaws that he admitted too. He kept his other defects hidden like a Leprechaun's pot of gold.

Maybelline make-up and mascara was smeared all over Haze's doll face after she forced herself to cry fake tears. Tears of joy were the only types of tears that were leaping from her Nasolacrimal duct. Haze was as synthetic as yaki weave from the beauty supply chains that only government hoes could afford.

In Chisel's misty mind, everybody was against him especially his wife Haze. How can a man still be sexually involved with a woman he distrusts? Guess pussy is pussy no matter how many miles it has on it. Still Chisel was waxing Haze's sweet ass through all of his daily suspicions like trust was optional. Sooner or later Chisel would learn the repercussions of thinking with his dickhead.

At a terrible time like this Haze was content with the way Chisel's life was crumbling down like his life just got whacked by a CAT Bulldozer. Now he was hurting the way she hurt every time he chose his liquid love over her feminine love. Now he would have to lose focus on their pending divorce and spend his energy and money on house hunting and getting himself back on his feet, but if she could she was going to do whatever it took to knock him down every time he was almost close to reestablishing himself. That was just what he got for marrying a Korean. His fault! Should've found somebody his own culture because he had no idea how Koreans operated even though they had been sexing for a year, engaged for another year, married after 3 years of life and love, in between that time their son sprouted about, and now they were separated.

It wouldn't be right if Haze didn't brag to one of her friends about how she set her husband up for failure so she called her good friend Kindle who often tricked with her when she wanted to double or triple her earnings.

Haze and Kindle met when Haze first migrated to the D and Kindle is the miscreant who introduced Haze to tricking. And Haze had the nerve to call Kindle "her friend." I guess they didn't teach her how to pick um in her homeland.

"Where the hell you been Haze?" Kindle answered who hadn't spoken with Haze in about a week which meant she had been up to no good.

"I've been around you know me. I got to keep the money flowing and keep myself going."

"Yeah I do so go ahead and spit it out. Tell me what you did now because I know you did something and you did something off the chains and that's why you're calling."

"Okay well I burned Chisel's house

45

down," Haze said with no hesitations.

"You're kidding me?"

"Nope I'm not kidding you."

"And who the hell gave you that bright idea? Wait, wait let me guess a light bulb? I hope you didn't burn his house down with him in it."

"Girl no, I don't want to kill the man I just want him to suffer. I was just thinking to myself what I could do to get him back for his alcoholic nature and that was the first thing that popped up in my head so I ran with it. Chisel and I got into a big nasty fight the other day. I had to do something big because he tried to rape me in front of our son."

"Why would he try to rape you in front of y'all son? You know you still be letting him tap that ass, and as many girls as he got

46

checking for him, I know he doesn't have a problem with getting some pussy."

"I'm telling you he picked my frail ass up, threw me all over his house like I was a bouncy ball or some shit, choked me up, had my legs spread open like an eagle's wings on the table, calling me all types of bitches and hoes, trying to pull my clothes off until I put his ass out."

"You mean to tell me you put him out his own house where he lives? The place that you Haze, don't live at anymore, the place that use to be your home?"

"I sure did."

"Your Korean ass is crazy. I sure hope your hands are clean momma."

"Of course I didn't burn his house down myself. I got a friend of a friend to do it for me."

"Yeah I bet, but it's time for me to hit the streets so I'll catch you on my downtime."

"Chow boo"

The statement birds of a feather flock together was very true about Haze and Kindle who were two money-hungry hookers at heart. After her and Haze got off the phone, Kindle went on a mission to score some major c-notes. Kindle's man of the hour went by the name of Rudy who was a neighborhood crack dealer and he made an agreement to pay her triple his usual pay if she came to his spot so he could get one off. Kindle was a five-star hooker and usually didn't work out a spot, but since the money was right, and her pockets needed to be refilled she agreed to just this one time.

Before Kindle and Rudy got busy,

Rudy had to make a sale and the buyer was no stranger. Unlike most men Kindle screwed, Rudy didn't think of her as a slut, and didn't mind paying her for his wants and needs. He felt it was just like giving your girl money to blow because him and Kindle were childhood friends and vowed to be friends to the end since they grew up on the same block. It was like breaking bread with family.

Since the buyer wanted more crack then what was in the front room stash, Rudy asked Kindle to bring him some more crack out the stash in his bedroom. Kindle knew exactly what area of his bedroom he was referring too because she played Rudy's sidekick in many other sales as well. And soon as she brought the crack out, she wished she would've said no and

stayed in the bedroom. Once she saw the

person standing before her looking like a feign,

she was never going to be the same again.

Nothing was ever going to be the same. Kindle

knew she was going to have to tell her homegirl

sooner or later the naked truth.

Chapter 4: Deal or No Deal

The night before the fire....

Last night Haze was a very, very naughty girl. She made a very selfless deal with the devil and his girlfriend. And the deal was she would give a street lord OJ and his girl Mesa a free threesome and pay them a grand total if he sent one of his soldiers to burn down her husband's house into a zillion smithereens.

Who and what would possess a madwoman to want to burn down her husband's house was a mystery. It wasn't like they had just separated and started having marital problems yesterday.

It's ironic how a person like Haze would give up her own hard-earned money and her body just to make a lethal deal as risky as a drug deal. And it's even more ironic how a person like Haze/supposed to be top notch Korean wasn't brave or bold enough to burn her husband's house down herself. Didn't she know the less people that knew the better? Obviously the streets in Korea weren't vehement enough to open up her eyes and there was no way OJ was just going to burn somebody's house down without asking any questions.

"Why do you want your husband's house burnt down? I mean you're a gorgeous woman. If your man doesn't want to do right by you that's his fault not yours. That means you need to find you somebody else because once the fire starts it ain't no turning back."

"Because I want revenge for all the pain he has caused me and my son. That man has more roller coasters then Cedar Point and the sad part about it is I still love him. Matter fact I can't stop loving him no matter how much I try to. And I damn sure didn't get married for nothing so the only way he's getting out of this marriage is in a bodybag."

"Obviously you want other men if you a hooker. I'm pretty sure you enjoy the pleasure just as much as you do the money," Mesa said up under her breath.

"So you don't want to kill him you just want his house to go up in flames?"

"Yeah that's correct."

"And how are we supposed to know if your husband isn't home?"

"His CTS Cadillac won't be parked in front of his 2-car garage." And even if no cars were visible in the front that didn't ensure that anybody wasn't home. What if Chisel let somebody borrow his car? Anything could go wrong.

"Well we don't patrol nobody houses we just make a hit and the hit is taken at the best time."

"So we got an understanding?"

"Yeah we got an understanding," OJ agreed with his eyes, but in his mind he had a whole nother plan.

OJ had been a regular consumer to Haze for a New York minute and just recently Mesa agreed to let him have the threesome he had been fantasizing for. Little did Haze know they had already chosen her to be their third-wheel they were just waiting on a golden opportunity. Never did they expect that Haze would proposition them and they would get paid in the process for a small favor. This would have to be the most ideal threesome ever.

Men and women were deeply attracted to Haze, and you would think her body would've reached its maximum potential by now with all the magic sticks it had triumphed, but it hadn't. It was something about being Korean that gave Haze a total advantage on her erotic lifestyle. No matter how many men or women she let navigate through her body, it never seemed to get *busted* like the average whore's twat does like her cookie was indeed one in a million. So her freaky ways began with OJ and his girl around nightfall when everyone was super high.

Haze started gazing enticingly at Mesa like she was candy on a stick.

"Bring your sexy ass on over here

Mesa so I can show you what I'm working with," Haze ordered Mesa who was already dressed in character. Immediately, that arrogant statement rubbed OJ the wrong way so he got up and flexed his hands around Haze's neck.

"Slow your role Haze that's my bitch. Don't be talking to her like you about to turn her out or something. I'm the only one who gives the commands around here. Are we clear? OJ clenched his grip around Haze's neck to let her know he wasn't joking," but instantly Haze nipples hardened up and her pussy began throbbing.

"Damn O, you know I like that kinky shit. Being choked turns me on but, get your hands off of my neck because your hands are only allowed to touch my titties, my clit, or my ass only so are we clear?"

"I don't want to hear no more talking. I want to see some action so close your mouth and go to work." OJ supervised Haze and Mesa and they did as they were told.

She began with French kissing as Haze cupped Mesa's perky breasts in a hypnotizing grasp, ass squeezing, panty dropping, finger twirling, clit tingling, and pussy dripping orgasms from both Haze and Mesa as OJ sat closely near jerking his dick back and forth to let his two lovely ladies know that it was their turn to turn the action onto his body so Haze teased OJ's long dick with a couple of lollipop licks. Then she began gobbling down his dick as he balanced himself by gripping the pinnacle of her head, taking a fistful of her hair and yanking it, and fucking her face while Mesa caressed and rubbed her soft, seductive skin. OJ let off one nut in Haze's mouth and she swallowed it like it was the normal thing to do when giving head.

"Yum that was delicious," Haze licked her lips and rolled her tongue forward for air. Instantly OJ got back rock hard again as he toyed with both Mesa and Haze at the same time so he could get ready for some elongated penetration.

At the end of the night, or should I say the middle of the morning everyone was sexually enthused. Haze dished out the grand, OJ pretended to set up the fire, and then Haze told her fuck buddies goodbye gladly like she had just made an innocent visit, when a day in her life was like a day in Pandora's Box.

No matter what Haze did, how she did

58

it, or who she did it with, it wasn't no shame in her game. I don't know how a person so internally filthy managed to sleep at night, but Haze did, and she managed to sleep like a newborn baby every night especially tonight.

Home for Haze seemed like it was in every open bed that was willing to blow money on their wildest fantasies, but it wasn't. Beachwood Apartments and Townhomes in Harrison Township was where she rested from her long, sweaty hooker days. Haze lived in a 2-bedroom townhome basically by herself. On the weekends when Haze wasn't tricking, her 3-year-old son her and Chisel shared lived there, but only on the weekends. On the weekdays little Chisel spent his time over Chisel's mother house since Haze didn't really have any other family in Michigan of her own.

The only people she could ever call family was Chisel's peoples. Little did she know Chisel's family hated her stinking guts, but they wasn't about to take their hate out on an innocent child so they smiled in her face and laughed behind her back.

Just as Chisel's house was blazing as the sun was coming up, Haze was dreaming; dreaming that her husband's house was on fire. I know you've heard of sleep-walking and sleep-talking, but Haze was actually smiling in her dream. Smiling so hard you would think she was taking a picture. In her dream one of OJ's soldiers fire bombed his house, and even though Chisel's house was indeed burning, it wasn't one of OJ's soldiers who committed the crime.

OJ and his girl Mesa pocketed the

grand she gave them last night because he didn't do family affairs. He wasn't an arsonist and certainly didn't know any arsonists even though he was a grimy man, a deal wasn't a deal in his book even if you shook hands, and he certainly didn't mix business up with pleasure because all Haze was pleasure. And it was no way he could do business with a hooker. No matter how pretty they looked or smart they seemed they weren't business material. OJ was a streetlord and if he had a problem with somebody he pulled a trigger and settled it. I know people say love makes you do some crazy things, but this thing that Haze was doing in the name of revenge was just spiteful and she was going to get exactly what she deserved for her evil deeds.

Chapter 5: Bull-Headed Mistress

The Infinite Impossibilities....

Weighing heavily on Mimosa's spirit, who was nicknamed Mo for short was the irresistible Chisel. For somebody who just came home from spending a wild night out with another man and for somebody whose pussy was still sore from last night's pounding, she had her nerve. Red passion marks were still laced all over her light toned body and she was reeking of Seagram's Vodka and dried up come. Even though Chisel was her main squeeze for now, it wasn't like Mo was cheating. How could she be cheating when the only person in this scenario who had some strings attached was Chisel? Mimosa may not be a cheater, but she was a downright hoe who managed to get herself caught up in Chisel's web of women just like all the other females he flaunted and taunted.

20-year-old Mimosa was being ratchet when she stumbled upon Chisel. Mo wanted some new dick in her life so she made herself a short and sweet intro on Livelinks, which was a local chat line local residents' used to meet bachelors and bachelorettes. Mo didn't even bother flirting with messages she went straight in for the kill.

"Mo wants to connect with you, so press the number one if you want to connect with her," Chisel was instructed by the lady coordinator and just like that Chisel connected. One sentence led to another, the two of them exchanged phone numbers, and after that one kiss led to another and Mo found herself parlaying naked in Chisel's bed.

Naively, Mo was trying to turn a sex affair into a real relationship with real feelings when she was still a side bitch. Side bitches always overstepped their boundaries. Side bitches never played their role. Even though she was half his mistress and half his lover according to his word and her mindset, she still had many limitations that she had to obey or was supposed to obey but, everyone knows mistresses love to get caught, they love breaking the rules, and are bull-headed when it comes to the demands of their companion in an effort to dignify they still have some brain cells in the chambers of their head that still work. I don't know how and why any woman would choose to settle.

"Hello," Mo thought it was Chisel calling her so she sprang to pick up her phone before she hopped in the shower to wash off all of her foul stenches.

"Mimosa Hayes, you have got to be the biggest hoe in Canada."

"Don't you mean America?"

"Don't correct me bitch let me finish."

"Who the fuck is this?"

"Bitch you know who it is and you not going to get away with what you did," a familiar voice swore through the phone.

"You can call me about fucking a nigga, but you can't call CPS about getting custody of your kids?"

"Bitch you late! I got all my kids back and I got a new man so you can have Limb's limp dick ass," Elise claimed angrily.

"So what are you calling me for then because we didn't just fall-out yesterday?"

"I'm warning you, you better stay away from my baby daddy."

"And I'm warning you, you better stay the fuck away from me before your ass be in the city morgue," Mo hung up.

The person she was feuding with was her ex-best friend Elise. First, Elise fucked Mo's baby daddy, then Mo returned the favor and fucked Elise's baby daddy. Elise's most recent baby daddy name was Limb and he had custody of their child while Elise's other two children remained lost in foster care. Elise was just calling Limb to come visit their daughter when she ended up with nothing, but an earful of aggravation when Limb started bragging about how he was smashing her friend, how he screwed her last night, and how her friend was going to be their daughter's stepmother.

Automatically, Elise knew that Limb was fucking Mimosa. It had to be her because Mimosa was the only slut that double fucked your leftovers. And there was no way in hell that Elise was going to let Mimosa play stepmother to her child.

On a scrapping level, Mo could beat the black off of Elise with her hands tied behind her back so it really wasn't even worth it. If Elise stepped to her on her turf, then that was going to be her fault, but Mo knew all Elise was trying to do was infuriate her which Mo wasn't going to let happen. She was going to get in the shower and go on with her day.

Endlessly, Mo had been calling Chisel all morning after she got out the shower. Even though it wasn't unordinary for him not to answer the phone, she could sense through her mistress senses that something was awfully wrong.

Luckily Mo just got finished facing a perfectly rolled KUSH blunt and chasing it with a Newport cigarette. The weed and nicotine mixture that had just been transmitted into her system was easing her paranoia a tad bit. Since her anxieties didn't subside she decided she would hop in her ride and do a drive-by.

Chisel lived about 25-35 minutes away from Mo's mother Roseville house. She hoped when she got there she would see his Caddy in its usual space parked near the garage. She would probably take a minute or two to decide if she would knock on his door knowing that he could have a sleazebag up in there or even worse his wife could be messing up her mistress time. Most likely, she would knock on his door because she had already been face to face with Haze before and wanted to snatch all her pretty cognac Korean hair from her scalp as she gave her a long-anticipated beat down. Didn't matter who was inside, long as she had some kind of justification from her sweetheart whether it be a quick glance or a text message to reassure her he was okay.

As Chisel's house was coming into plain view, Mo couldn't believe her observations. She hoped she was hallucinating and she made a wrong turn through her course somewhere, but she didn't. She was in his city, she was on his street, and she was figuratively confused. She felt completely bamboozled by her surroundings. How could this be? It wasn't even a house anymore, it was a nightmare. She tried to hold back the water works, but she failed because they were running down her face faster and faster. Now her anxieties were even worse then what they were when she decided to take this inconclusive journey over here.

Mo was a little relieved when she realized Chisel's Caddy was nowhere near the premises, but still that didn't mean anything. In all honesty, Mo wanted to get out her car and do some investigating of her own. She wanted to search through what was left of Chisel's house even though her body would carry on an aroma of smoke and she would probably mess up her brand new UGG boots in the process of searching. None of that would prevent her from making sure the man of her dreams body wasn't in the debris except for reality.

Sitting slumped in front of Chisel's house Mo took her phone and starting taking snapshots and screenshots of Chisel's house. She took 3 of her best shots and turned those 3 single pictures into a collage.

The caption read "this is why you don't cheat because a bitch might mess around and burn down your shit."

Mo felt like this fire was related to Karma, cheating, infidelity, and whatever else Chisel was doing behind the dark including her. So Mo tweeted, Instagrammed, and Facebooked her morning sorrow like social networking was going to bring Chisel back or something when all it was really doing was putting a magnifying glass up to your business and giving people an invitation to comment on your life.

Unable to think of any friends or family members she knew of Chisel's, because Mo had driven all of his friends away, and didn't associate with any of his family members so that was a negative. She thought about circling the block most of his boys usually hang on, but they probably could give a penny about Chisel's house burning down, and she would probably only find herself slapping somebody today because every time Chisel left the room, his boys would be all over her, and would try to get her at all costs.

While driving around the vicinity a little bit longer not ready to go home and face all the infinite possibilities that were trailing through her mind Mo double-checked her phone. Apparently, she had 100 likes on her collage and 30 comments all that she was going to deal with when she got home. Damn social networks worked fast.

Running out of options, Mo decided to call the nearest fire station to see if she could get some valuable info out of them, but after calling them ten times and not getting an answer she knew that it was a wrap until she felt like trying again. Guess the fire department only worked in 911 situations and to Mo this was a 911 situation, a cold blue, a flat line situation, whatever you wanted to call it.

On the way home tears were flowing everywhere left and right across her face when disaster decided to strike like heavy lightning with raining and thundering once again as if her day needed any more tragedy.

As Mo was getting ready to zoom in her driveway, she couldn't because the red, white, and blue boys were blocking her entrance so she ended up parallel parking in front of her house. Oblivious as to what two police officers were doing on her property, she got out of her car to explore the possibilities. The two cops were in the back of her house by her bedroom, so Mo sprinted to the back of her house by her bedroom with her house keys in hand. When Mo saw a trail of broken glass on the grass from her 2 bedroom windows, she began shouting all kinds of obscenities.

"Oh my fucking God! Dirty motherfuckers! This is some true life bullshit! I don't have time to be playing Mrs. Fix It right now!"

"Ma'am calm down so we can figure out what happened," the officers tried to pacify the situation.

The bust job was very unusual because the window-breakers didn't use bricks, nothing was stolen, and they targeted Mo's bedroom windows as if the shit was personal. And Mo's neighbor to the right being the patron he was and hearing the car screeches and the glass shatter he heard while he was messing around in his back yard called the police.

Who would want to bust Mo's window? All she could think about was how she was going to explain this one to her mother. Explain was not the word because once she revealed to her mother two of her windows were broken she wasn't going to be able to explain anything and was probably going to be permanently evicted from her mother's residence. Mo wished she could make this go away before her mom got home from work, but she didn't know anybody that fixed broken windows or would fix a broken window for a fix of her so she was out of luck. Thank God no one was home when this happened and no one was chilling in Mo's bedroom because it would've been an ambulance accompanying the single, unmarked squad car.

"Was this your bedroom ma'am?" A policeman who was freely dressed asked Mo as she stood lethargically in the backyard. This policeman was dressed in True Religion jeans with a police badge safety pinned to his North Face fleece. While one officer questioned Mo with his handy dandy notebook, the other officer studied the surroundings looking for clues.

"This was my bedroom," Mo responded

"Well do you know who did this or anybody who would do something like this?" And as she opened her closed mind, she recalled just arguing with Elise over the phone. Elise had never done anything like this before and it is certainly unlikely she became big and bad in a couple of hours. Even though she knew better to never put anything past a bitch, she couldn't be sure so she didn't throw her up under the bus just yet.

"Not right now, but I need to call my mother and let her know what happened so would it be alright if we came down to the station to file a report whenever she comes home?"

"Yes that would be fine, but do you mind letting us collect whatever evidence you have in your bedroom that broke your two windows because we're going to need it for evidence. We can dust it for fingerprints so we can find out who did this awful crime." Mo could tell the officers really didn't give a damn about finding out who broke her 2 bedroom windows. They were just doing what they usually did on working hours which was randomly selecting people to fuck with, and pretending to give a damn whenever they were called on the scene.

"Whatever just make it quick." So Mo hurried up and unlocked her front door while the officer stood basically on her heels. And since he was the last person coming in, he locked the door behind them. Mo's front door had a loud lock and a loud shut so immediately she dug in her purse to retrieve her Tootoo which was a nickname for her pocket knife that always came in handy in crazy situations.

"What are you doing? Can you get what you need and leave please?" Mo said wanting the police to hurry up and get away from her house because her house had enough attention already with yellow tape stretched around it.

"I can, but first I think we can make a deal. I can help you if you help me," the officer claimed pressing his body up against Mo's so she moved back as far back as she could away from the con.

"And people say the police are supposed to honor and protect. The only way you can help me is by getting out of my house before you get cut." And just as the strange man was about to take Mo into his kinky world of pleasure, one of her sisters came in and saved her. And as much as she loved rough sex

and making side deals to get what she wanted
this was not the time or the place.

"You can file that report later ma'am.
Now you have a good day," the officer stated
as he made a quick exit without even retrieving
what he was supposed to retrieve.

"Dirty motherfuckers," Mo muttered to
herself.

Chapter 6: Moaning off the Hinges

Tonight I'll be your naughty girl…

Police veteran Wiley Woodward was having the worst day of his investigator life. Crime after crime, he never seemed to get a break.

What he thought was going to be a peaceful, hot lunch at his empty house in his empty kitchen was simply wishful thinking. Wiley slid his Stouffer's Chicken Alfredo meal in the microwave for 5 minutes. He grabbed a Country Time Lemonade out the fridge, turned on some Judge Mathis, and hiked his feet up on his foot rest. Loud, sexual noises filled the supposed to be empty air.

"What the fuck is that?" Wiley thought to himself knowing that whatever he was hearing wasn't just going to pop out at him. He

decided to go searching and follow those noises. It's a shame that even at home he had to solve shit. As he got closer and closer to his daughter's room, he couldn't believe the climatic sounds that were disturbing his fatherly ears.

"Oh Terrace, oh, oh, oh!" Angel screamed. Wiley hoped and prayed that somebody had broken and entered into his home to use his daughter's bed as a temporary bachelor pad.

"Say my name Angel?" Terrace spoke. Wiley's hopes were now extinguished by the truth. His daughter was a freak-a-leak and she was busy with a meeting in her bedroom with Terrace. He should've stuffed a pillow on top of Angel's face to silence her moans and groans.

. Still fully equipped in his authoritative uniform, Wiley's police belt was full of weapons he could be selective with. And out of all his weapons he withdrew his gun out like he was about to make an arrest and banged on Angel's door.

"Angel, what is going on?" Wiley yelled, but there was no response. Angel didn't hear her daddy's voice echo at all.

"Look if I got to bust in there it's not going to be nice so I advise you two to answer me right now because I'm aimed and trained to shoot and mangle." Still there was no response so Wiley stood back, cocked his leg up, and kicked her door down. And when Angel heard her door fall off the hinges she knew it was her Wiley's doing. This time she wanted to explain herself, but she couldn't talk because it was duck tape strapped over her mouth.

Wiley had his gun pointed at both Angel and her boyfriend Terrace who we're butt ass naked, but lucky they were wrapped up in dark green cotton sheets. Prior to this slick teenage encounter, Wiley had only met Terrace once before. No matter what kind of picture Angel tried to paint about her guiltless boyfriend, Wiley didn't like anything about Terrace at all, not even his name.

Terrace and Angel had just gotten back together after breaking up and now their relationship was certainly going to be OVER. Wiley really didn't know what to do when he saw Angel because she looked like a victim laying there in her bed, in her room with tape over her mouth, but she couldn't be a victim. Her arms were free and so was she, but what was going on in her twisted young mind to let somebody practically suffocate her was the question? On the other hand, Wiley couldn't let himself believe that his sweet little angel had gone bad. No matter how things looked he was on her side all the way and could only see his daughter as his little princess whether she was wrong or right. He just knew there was no way Angel would conjure up something like this on her own even though she did. It didn't even ring in his head that Angel was skipping school, Angel told Terrace to come over here, and Angel opened up the door to let Terrace in. Instead the only thing that rung in his head was Angel was innocent.

"What did you do to my daughter? You know what doesn't matter because you will never hurt her again and you probably will never see her again after this." Wiley pulled his trigger back, checked his aim, and released a bullet out of his gun chamber. It struck Terrace right in his left shoulder blade from the back, and Angel almost screamed the tape off her mouth, but the sudden shooting was enough for her to finally rip the tape off her.

"What the hell is wrong with you Wiley? Put your stupid gun away! Last time I checked this was my room and you were supposed to knock before you entered!" Neither Terrace nor Wiley could believe the words that were falling out of Angel's mouth. Even though they were caught in the act for disrespecting Wiley's roof, Angel was not remorseful at all.

"I don't know what you do at your mother's house, but you're not going to do that shit here Angel or you can get the fuck out with your company."

"I'm not going anywhere Wiley. You're stuck with me and I'm stuck with you until my mother returns."

"So this is what you like to do in your spare time? You like being a little slut? You think this clown isn't going to fuck you and leave you?"

"No, I don't love clowns, but you do Wiley. Delilah was a clown, and that's exactly why she fucked you, she married you, and left you for all of your savings."

"Shut up Angel," Wiley commanded.

"You shouldn't have done that Mr. Woodward." Terrace asserted confused at who was in trouble in this situation because Angel and her daddy were going at it. Since Terrace had been shot before and thought he was a thug at heart, he was silently hurting. He just took his t-shirt and wrapped his shoulder up as tight as he could to put pressure on his open wound and began clothing himself."

"What you gonna do call your goons on me? I got goons too. And if you tell anybody anything about this I will find you and kill you."

"And now you're threatening me?"

"You won't win in this system man especially not against me because I know all the people that run this city. Your trespassing on my property, you were causing bodily harm to my daughter, and I already know you got a criminal record and warrants so I'm pretty sure you don't want to go to the authorities on me because I already ran a background check on you and your family so you listen hear and you listen good. You better stay the fuck away from my daughter, get the hell up out of my house, and keep this bullet between us or else it will be many more of where those came from."

Angel ran to the bathroom making sure she held her sheet super tight so Wiley wouldn't be exposed to all her teenage goodies as if catching his daughter screwing somebody in his house wasn't exposure enough. She had to flee the room before Terrace and her sperm contributor began exchanging words so she blocked their conversation out of her head. Angel's thoughts were everywhere but, she wasn't even fazed about being caught. She was about to go nuts because her boyfriend just got shot right in front of her face and her sperm donor pulled the trigger.

"We're about to take a ride," Wiley directed Terrace as he bully shoved Terrace out of his house.

"I don't want to take no ride with you. You the FEDS and you shot me man. Blood is about to be everywhere. Go push somebody else around."

"You should've thought about that before you put your paws on my daughter. Now get your ass in the back before I take your little young ass to jail."

"Take me to jail for what giving your daughter some of my sweet loving?"

"Don't flatter yourself." Wiley took Terrace's head, made sure he purposefully hit it on the car's roof, opened the back door for him, and threw him on the backseat.

"This is police brutality!"

As Wiley was preparing to scare the living shit out of Terrace, and was proceeding to the nearest hospital, his high speed chase pace was interrupted by another Clinton Township crime.

"Chief Woodward there has been a woman's burnt body found on the 1300 block of Glenwood Avenue, between Harper Road and Gratiot Avenue. Please report their immediately."

"Copy that," Wiley spoke through his radio sync.

Remembering Terrace was still in the backseat of his ride, Wiley knew he had to get rid of Terrace and get rid of Terrace quick so he pulled a quick move.

"Jump out!"

"Are you crazy man this is a moving

vehicle?"

"Yes I'm crazy and I got crimes to solve, so we'll finish this later."

"What the fuck did I get myself into?" Terrace asked himself before he opened up his back door and rolled himself onto the pavement trying not to injure himself more than what he was already injured.

***

Fortunately for Mo her neighbor Zee told her he could go to Habitat for Humanity and grab her 2 bedroom windows, and install them for her and whenever she got the money she could repay him later. The only reason Zee came up with such a considerate gesture was because he was very close with Mo's mother and he knew that she was heavily stressed and balling on a budget. Mo's mother was trying to do the best that she could and was practically

working herself to death everyday to pay the

bills. Mo's mother couldn't afford anymore

downfalls, letdowns, or loans. So Zee helped

Mo clean up her old glass, and replaced her

bare windows with new windows. Most likely,

Mo's mother was going to come in from work

and not notice one single thing different.

As far as filing the report, Mo was

going to have to do that her damn self. It wasn't

like police were going to be in a hurry to solve

anything anyway when there were fraudulent

people robbing banks and serial killers on the

loose. Whenever she got some quality time out

of her mistress-filled days, she was going to

have to put two and two together and decide

who was linked to her two broken bedroom

windows. Frankly, a bitch had to do it. Who's

bitch and for what reason was the question.

Chapter 7: From Ashes to Dust

High off of life...

The desperation for a quick consumption of sweet, sharp liquor was blowing Chisel's un-blown mind. Money was also on Chisel's mind too. He hadn't landed any basketball contracts in a while and he was beginning to feel like he was drying out his own bank accounts. Just when Chisel was about to consider getting a job, he received an email for a private appearance. The Detroit Pistons were having a basketball luncheon at Jay Alexander's in West Bloomfield Hills and they wanted Chisel to be their guest speaker. People admired the way Chisel spoke in group settings because he spoke concisely and his messages were always as powerful as a prophet. Although, Chisel had multiple barriers going on in his life he still didn't feel like a hypocrite or intimidated from speaking to a group of successful men about life, basketball, and success. He would do anything for a check. How can you beat getting paid five grand just for giving a 10 minute speech, wearing a nice tailored suit, putting on a fake smile, handing out a couple of handshakes, and eating lunch with fellow basketball idols.

Chisel was honored to keep feeling the love of basketball even though he was washed up and played out, and he never even played professional basketball in the United States except for high school basketball. As far as basketball performers were concerned a rookie didn't have shit on a MVP (most valuable player).

So what the hell why not take one for

the team? On the way to Chisel's luncheon he stopped at one of his regular liquor stores, talked a little shit to the counter boys, and bought him 2 cold double shots of Extra Smooth Vodka. One he gobbled down in his car as he sped off to West 696 and the other one he was saving for later. Hopefully, nobody smelled Vodka on his breathe, but even if they did oh well because Chisel was stuck in his ways and it was nothing that no one preacher or wise man could say to change that.

***

In the middle of Wiley's thoughts his boss dropped another case on his desk as if his caseload wasn't already heavy. As Wiley did a quick review of the case he learned that the suspected crime was "arson" but the kind of arson was the question, and the victim's house

98

was Chisel Simmons on the 40000 block of Rivergate Drive. He was no stranger to the penitentiary, probation, or drug charges, but this time he was on the right side of the law, but like they say presumed innocent until proven guilty.

This case was going to be very tricky. There were no dead bodies found at the scene, and the scene itself was nothing, but ashes and dust so it was going to be pretty hard to gain something from a scene of dead smoke. And according to the file there was one witness on the scene when authorities arrived there who hadn't given her statement, but left her name and three contact numbers which included her house number, her cell number, and her work number where she could be reached which made Wiley raise his eyebrows. Who leaves three different contact numbers to be reached by the police of all people? The answer is *no one except someone who has strong motives against someone else and really wants them to rot away.*

Her name was Cyn Clarkson, and since the first number on the file was her cell phone number he called it first. (Ring, ring.)

"Hello."

"Yes is this Cyn Clarkson?"

"Sure is."

"This is Police Chief Wiley Woodward calling regarding the Chisel Simmons case. Do you have a few minutes to speak with me?"

"Yes I do."

"Well the quicker I can get you into the station to give your statement the quicker I can be out of your hairs. So do you have time today to come in?"

"I really want you to hurry up and close this case to, but I can't make it today."

"Wish I got more witnesses like you everyday so when are you free to come in?"

"Tomorrow is good for me, how about you?"

"That's perfect say tomorrow around noon?"

"See you then." Right after Cyn closed her phone up she got to doing the Brandy bounce, praising, and clapping her hands because tomorrow was her day to shine where she could finally get everything she wanted in this world, just with a simple confession it was her destiny to give.

Cyn, another one of Chisel's light skin bombshells had a long line of hate towards

Haze and it was solely Chisel's fault, but a woman never wants to blame the man for his wrongdoing. It's only normal to blame the woman and give her hell. When Cyn and Chisel got together, Chisel gave her the "I'm separated from my wife story waiting to get a divorce," which was partially true at the time. Chisel did have future intentions of making Cyn his main chick until Cyn pulled her gun out on him in his sleep. Cyn's nosy ass was lurking through Chisel's phone and she found a bunch of incriminating evidence that she should've never saw and wasn't supposed to see. Knowing that she wasn't about to be cheated on ever again by no man, Cyn had to set the record straight so she pulled out her silver piece and aimed it for Chisel's head. And she held it between his closed eyeballs until he woke up.

"What the fuck are you doing Cyn? Get that thing up out of my face! I told you I didn't want your ass to get your CCW."

"And I told you I didn't want to be cheated on, but I guess you didn't understand that." Cyn held her pistol in her left hand and waved Chisel's phone in her right hand.

"I'm sorry Cyn, I'm just not cut out for this relationship thing. I've really been thinking a lot and I've been thinking I mine as well fix things with my wife. I already cheated on her a thousand times anyway."

"Good you be with your wife because Cyn isn't going out like that." And just like that Cyn left Chisel all the way alone, but revenge was a dish that was best served cold. She made sure she kept her ammunition ready for her strike because Haze was to blame. Tomorrow Police Chief Wiley Woodward was going to be her new best friend because she had a package deal for him that came with evidence, a testimony, and a description.

***

Angel loved making her sperm giver go nuts, and wanted somebody to console her ASAP like Remy Martin VSOP so she grabbed her phone, scrolled through her contacts, and picked the first person that came to her wet mind who was Eon. Eon was a cop trainee, who Wiley was mentoring three days a week. If only Wiley would've thought twice about bringing Eon around his daughter, but he never thought no one that he worked with would cross those lines. Little did Wiley know that when he brought Eon to his home and introduced Eon and Angel, Eon made sure before he left Wiley's house to slide Angel his direct number. And just like that Eon and Angel became phone and texting buddies. Angel figured she mine as well give him a buzz since Wiley told Eon her personal business anyway.

"How's my little angel doing?" Eon answered.

"Your little angel is not doing too good because she just got caught up by the warden of the house."

"Tell me what happened Angel. You know I love listening to your stories."

"Wiley caught me and my boyfriend fucking in my room."

"That's it? That's what all the commotion is about?"

"There's more, but I don't care to say. I called to see what's good with you and what you doing today?"

"Your dad blew me off so I'm not going to be training with him today, but I would love to make my way to see you," Eon flirted.

"So why don't you come over right now while it's still early."

"You not saying nothing, but a word baby girl. I hope you ready because I'm on my way." Eon had been waiting for weeks to get his statutory hands on Angel, and today was going to be his lucky day. Clearly, her boyfriend didn't finish his job so Eon was going to finish it for him.

Chapter 8: You turning me off

The Best Night I Never Had

Mo's face lit up like a light bulb when she saw Chisel's number finally pop up on her screen. She hoped this wasn't his wife calling trying to check her about the "fire" or one of his family members or friends calling to confirm Chisel's tragic death, but it was only one way for her to get the closure she had been yearning so she answered.

"Hello."

"Yeah bay what you doing?" Mo was finally exalted that Chisel finally decided to grace her ears with his voice.

"I'm not doing nothing just posted up at the crib."

"I bet you thought I was dead didn't you?"

"Of course I didn't. That was the last thing I wanted to think. I've been trying to think positively. I'm dying to know what happened because I drove by your house today and I practically lost my mind."

"All I know is that somebody fire-bombed my house."

"Why would somebody want to fire-bomb your house Chisel?" Remembering the scene Mo believed that was a good explanation, but she knew there was way more to the story then what he was admitting.

"I don't know Mo how do I know you didn't get mad at me and fire-bomb my house?"

"That's not even in my character Chisel."

"I hope not."

"How do I know that you didn't do no insurance job on your house? Wouldn't be the first time I heard something like this happening out of the blue."

"I didn't do no damn insurance job," Chisel snapped.

"You know you can tell me what really happened I'm not going to tell nobody." *That's what they all say Chisel thought to himself.*

"So who do you think did it?"

"I really don't know. I don't have any enemies, but I suspect it was probably a friend of a friend." Mo didn't know what Chisel meant by that, but she hoped his suspicion wasn't resting on one of her friends. It was certainly time to change the subject.

"Anyways get dressed, I'm about to come get you, and we about to crash the Crazy

Horse." Mo was always down for whatever as long as she was with her boo nothing else mattered. As far as she was concerned women should spend more time doing what their men love to do even if they wanted to do things like going to the strip club.

It's been a minute since Mo and Chisel were out together in the public eye so tonight she had to look extra sexy. Little did she know that she was about to get the shockwave of her irrational life.

Quickly, Mo put on some make-up, freshened up, and put on a fresh thong. She threw on her tightest jeans, made sure her Brazilian weave was straight, her cleavage was right, and zipped up her favorite black stiletto thigh high boots. Before she knew it, Chisel let her know he was outside. She just knew her and Chisel were going to have some private time after the Crazy Horse and she wasn't going to come creeping in until the next afternoon. As she got closer and closer to his ride, she noticed that somebody was already sitting in her seat on the passenger side of Chisel.

What the fuck is going on? Last time I checked I didn't sign up to be nobody's third wheel. Chisel is always on some slick ass bullshit. I thought it was just going to be me and him like the good old days, but I guess I was wrong. He's always spoiling our fun. That's exactly why I never take his ass seriously.

Once Mo was all the way in the backseat, she realized the other person in the passenger seat where she was supposed to be sitting was Chisel's wife. Automatically, Mo wanted to roll down her window and vomit. She wanted to mangle Chisel like an Asiatic lion mangles a wildebeest for dinner. She wanted to stick Chisel with extremely thin needles all over his body like acupuncture on some Final Destination type of shit. She wanted to kill Chisel for bringing her around his cunt of a wife like she was meaningless.

I mean really what kind of idiot brings his wife to his mistress's house? Never bring a bitch to my house and never acknowledge in my face that you are fucking with another bitch even if you are. I'm supposed to always feel like I'm the only girl in your world even if I'm not. Point is you should never let me feel differently.

As bad as Mo wanted to get out of the

car at the next red light or tell her 2-party posse to turn the Caddy around and take her back home, she decided to stay.

Off to the Crazy Horse they went with a very intense conversation. The whole car was tense and Haze was making everything worst with her superiority level because even a blind man can see she felt like she had the upper hand.

"So what's your name again girl?" Haze asked Mo even though she knew her name. Haze just quizzically stared at Mo through her sun visor mirror.

"You know damn well what my name is so don't front because everybody knows how raunchy you really are." Mo blasted back.

"I'm raunchy, that was cute, but if anybody in this car is raunchy it's you for fucking a married man." Mo's face was legendary. She didn't know if Haze was using that as a rebuttal or she knew the truth.

"What I'm no fool, I know y'all fucking. Y'all can play that friend shit with me all your want, but I can see it in your eyes little girl."

"Both of y'all bitches can eat a dick. I love both of y'all and were about to go out and have some fun whether y'all like it or not. Haze you know that Mo is just my friend so stop tripping. Remember whose driving. If you didn't want to come with me to get Mo you shouldn't have, but you did. That's your fault. I just had a major tragedy happen to me and I thought just maybe I could drink my pain away with my two favorite ladies." Mo didn't know what Chisel was on right now, but he was really mentally retarded in the head. When did she become "his friend" as he put it because last time she checked she was more than just a friend and they were planning to be together forever. And did he think Mo was suppose to pretend that she liked Haze just to have a couple of drinks like this was Barney and Friends or something and everybody had to be cool because it wasn't. Mo was a force not to be reckoned with and Chisel should've known better then to try to put them two together.

Luckily, Haze left Chisel and Mo alone at the bar leading them to think it was just about to be about the two of them, but she knew Chisel was about to get wasted and it would only be minutes before he came running to her rescue from a pack of men.

The DJ was banging "Pour It Up" by

Rihanna and Haze went to check out one of the Crazy Horse dancers alone work her private silver pole. "Throw it up, throw it up," like Rihanna said in her song, Haze threw a bunch of one's at the sexy stripper who was making her booty clap just for Haze. Being that Haze use to do a little stripping in her time before she traded it in for hooking, Haze felt like she was at home and could appreciate a talented dancer with admirable body language. The stripper whose name was Rosé pulled Haze up on her stage and they began putting on a show for all of the Crazy Horse's thirsty men.

Chisel swallowed shot after shot not even paying any attention to Mo who was watching Haze show off and show out.

"I guess that bitch thinks she cute, but I bet if all the men up in here knew what I knew about her, they would be laughing at her ass right now calling her nasty, and would be planning to run trains on her at the end of the night at the closest motel." Chisel didn't even say anything about Mo's comment so she started snapping her fingers in his face.

"Knock, knock anybody home?"

Mo was trying to conversate with Chisel who just ignored her and staggered his drunk self off sideways trailing through the crowd to confront all the horney men that were surrounding his wife and her new lady friend who just laughed at him and began beating him. Unlike everybody else who was rushing to the scene to see the fight, a fight in Mo's head meant "time to go" so she left the bar as fast as she could.

"That's what his stupid ass gets for

being so messy. I would go save him, but since he tried to put me on the back-burner for the bitch that I'm supposed to be replacing, he can let that bitch save him. I don't even care if I speak to his drunken ass again. And Mo didn't even get to confide in him about how she thought Haze might've broken her 2 bedroom windows. She said fuck that shit too. As far as she was concerned those two cornballs belonged together."

Right now home was the place to be and Mo couldn't wait to get home so she could wake up and forget about the worst night she ever had out on the town. Even though Mo was in her thigh-high boots and it was only right for her ride to take her home, she was going to find her own damn way home because it surely wasn't to be from Chisel who was getting beat-up and beat down. About to hit Michigan Ave, Mo knew she wouldn't be walking anywhere for long because she was never alone for long anyway.

"Aye Mo, hold up baby girl." Stopping in her tracks and turning around to see who knew her name, Mo caught eyes with her biggest crush which was a guy named Donnie. Everybody in the hood knew Donnie was in love with her and so did Mo, but she didn't care. Just like a bald-headed female to ignore the guys that really like you and only pay attention to the guys who dog her out and treat her like shit, but tonight there was a different glare in her eyes like she was starting to wake up and smell the black coffee.

"Hey Donnie, what are you doing here?"

"I was just leaving and by the looks of it so were you so you need a ride home or anything?"

"Actually I do."

"So let's go."

Little did Mo and Haze know that the people that were attacking there precious Chisel knew him very well and were beating him for reasons far worse than the eye could perceive. This wasn't just your average bar fight over a hot chick it was much more and eventually both Mo and Haze were going to find out exactly what that fight was truthfully about.

Chapter 9: The Bitch Confesses

Ain't no dirt up under my fingernails...

I never knew anybody so cooperative or so thrilled to drive past a police station let alone go inside it, and be so comfortable about snitching, except for Cyn who had a hidden agenda. Cyn was treating this police encounter like she was going on an interview. She dressed herself very sophisticated, was well-prepared, and even arrived at the station early with a newspaper knowing she hated reading, and especially hated reading newspapers. She signed herself in and sat down in a seat closest to the entry where all the waiting people seemed to be escorted through making sure she kept a humongous smile on her face, and smiled and waved at everyone. Finally Wiley called her name.

A minute after noon, the games were certainly about to begin. And in Cyn's mind this was a day worth waiting for and this was a speech worth giving.

"Mrs. Clarkson I'm Police Chief Wiley Woodward, but please call me Wiley. I've been working with this department for over 15 years so you're in good hands," the fine detective introduced himself on the way back to his village.

"It's a pleasure to meet you in person Wiley please call me Cyn," Cyn gave the chief goggily eyes. After going through a bunch of loops, stairs, and hallways Cyn was exactly where she wanted to be. Sitting alone, right in front of Mr. Woodward about to spill her guts out in a solitary room which most would be sweating bullets and feeling like they was in a dungeon. She was in complete bliss and didn't feel out of place not one bit.

"I hope the walk wasn't too long. I should've told you to wear sneakers," Wiley joked as the click clacking of Cyn's pumps finally silenced.

"It wasn't too long at all. Unlike most girls I can do anything and go anywhere in these pumps without never being in any discomfort."

"Can I get you anything before we start? Some water, a cup of black coffee, some cocoa, or some tea?"

"No thank you I am fine as you can see."

"Well let's begin." Wiley got his yellow pad and pen ready, sat his tape recorder right side up and pressed RECORD. The beginning of the tape started off with a brief introduction of Cyn. Cyn revealed her full name was Cyn "Irae" Clarkson, she was 24 years of age, a Detroit native, and she use to be romantically involved with Chisel Simmons.

"So tell me what do you know about the fire?"

"I know the fire wasn't an accident and it certainly wasn't due to any electrical failure. Haze who is Chisel's wife has had a very strong vendetta against Chisel since he told her he wanted to separate and divorce so Haze has been determined to find something she could do to turn the tables because if Chisel and her got a divorce she would lose everything. More then what Chisel lost in the fire."

"Aren't you the one who called 911 about this fire?"

125

"Yes I am."

"If Chisel stays in Clinton Township and you live in Detroit, what were you doing at Chisel's house?"

"I work in Clinton Township near his home. I've been driving past his house and checking on him every since I heard about him and Haze's volatile relationship. I just be making sure he's okay. I don't want to see anything bad happen to him."

"So you lied on your 911 call when you told dispatchers you were a neighborhood resident, Chisel was out of town, and you knew nobody was home, You didn't know none of this."

"I did what I had to do to get help."

"Do you honestly think if I would've said yes my baby daddy house is on fire, I was just driving by 911 would've responded as quickly?"

"I guess that makes sense."

"Check this out then." First piece of evidence Cyn handed Wiley to back up her story was a copy of Haze's birth certificate which she managed to confiscate from Chisel's house one day when she was searching through a box of their important papers. She knew it was going to come in handy one day. His fault for having his wife's certificate mixed up in the clutter.

"As you see Haze is Korean and was born in Korea which would make her an illegal immigrant so to solve this error Chisel agreed to marry Haze so she could live here, but if they get a divorce obviously Haze would be shipped and handled back to Korea where she came from with their kid, and he would probably never see his kid again because it was no way in Hades he was going to Korea. You can call immigration for yourself because you're a cop and you can do those things. I'm just a girl trying to prove my point."

Secondly, Cyn played a phone recording for Wiley featuring the alleged Haze speaking recklessly about setting a fire.

"Three days before the fire I went over Chisel's house to pick up my son and Haze was there. I asked her where Chisel was and she told me that he had stepped out. She said he couldn't wait any longer and had something important to do. As I was gathering my son's things and putting on his hat, coat, and gloves, Haze kept telling me. *I hope you don't have anything important here because next time you come here, this house isn't going to be here.* I knew she wasn't just talking crazy so I pulled out my phone and tried to see exactly what she was talking about. Soon as the conversation started I hit RECORD so I asked her was Chisel getting evicted or something and she responded of course not you know he pays the bills. I'm just going to blow this house down that's all." There wasn't nothing in Haze's voice to say she was playing. She wasn't intoxicated and she wasn't high. She knew exactly what she was saying and she meant it.

"So chief after hearing the words come out the horse's mouth herself are you honestly going to tell me it was just a coincidence of her saying she was going to blow his house down and three days later the house catches on fire?"

"I'm not going to point any fingers yet,

129

but I'm starting to get the feeling she did set this fire or she was an accessory."

"Well I'm not finish I've got more."

Thirdly, Cyn handed Wiley a copy of an illegal stripper's license with Haze's face stamped all over it.

"As you see someone made Haze a fake stripper's license since she can't get a real job here because she's not a U.S. citizen. Stripping and hooking were the only things she could really do under the table so that's exactly what she did. For somebody whose from out of the country, who didn't have any family here, but all of these scandalous friends you would have to assume she was very sneaky and persuasive because she got a stranger into making her stripper l's. Why couldn't she get someone to blow up her husband's house for the right

130

price? Not to mention you know the kinds of people strippers and hookers come across. I've seen her and she is one of the most stunning Korean women I have seen, so I'm pretty sure she knows how to use her body to her advantage since that's what she does all day every day. And you should call her son's babysitter and ask her how long she watches Haze's son because if you knew what I knew you would certainly see Haze as an unfit mother, who really wasn't fazed about the responsibility she held to her son. I don't know what she's going to tell her son when he finds out his mother is a hooker. To Haze this fire was nothing but, a way for her to redeem herself because once Chisel found out she was a tramp he could never look at Haze the same and he began drinking obsessively."

"So how do I know you don't have a strong vendetta against Haze and aren't just trying to get her out the way so you can have Chisel all to yourself?" Cyn had to snicker off that one because the chief was way off with his assumptions. It was true Cyn did have a vendetta against Haze and wanted to see her locked up behind bars, but none of this was about Chisel, and all her testimony did have a lot of truth in it. It was all about Cyn coming out on top making sure that at the end of the day Haze understood that just because she may have won the battle, she lost the war.

"Chief, if I wanted Chisel I could have him. I'm the one who broke off the relationship, but to me you can't even call what we had a relationship because it is impossible for a man to have a relationship with two women. Chisel had been selling me excuses for the past three years I've known of how he was going to divorce his wife and I just got tired of waiting so I moved on." Cyn waved her ring finger in the air to display a 24-karat ring on her ring finger that symbolized she was engaged. Too bad the only person she was engaged to was herself, but it wasn't a crime in pretending to be someone's fiancé.

"The evidence is right in front of your face. I'm not making any of this up. I don't have anything to gain by giving Haze up to you (which was a lie). Not to mention me and Haze are actually good friends (which was an even bigger lie). My son could've been in that house when she set it on fire, and my son could've lost his father because of this so no I don't want to see Haze get away with an intentional crime."

"Okay well this just about wraps it up so I'm going to look into all the information you gave me and I'll be getting back with you in a couple of days to let you know the status of this case." Cyn made sure to side-track Wiley as much as she could so he wouldn't be able to ask her investigator protocol questions. And she should really pat herself on the back when she got a chance because she did a job well done.

"That sounds good to me. I hope to hear from you soon. Please show me the way out I don't remember all those twists and turns."

"I sure can." Once Cyn hit the parking lot, she hoped that Wiley was as intelligent as he looked and would persecute Haze to the fullest extent just as she had convicted her and persecuted her in her mind. All the evidence Cyn presented forward was strong, and made her look like she was pursuing a law major or watched too much Law TV because she came fully-loaded with more than just a confession. She had hardcore evidence and she made Wiley completely aware of Haze's motive. To her life was good, but it was only going to get better.

Chapter 10: Angel Eyes

There's nothing angelic about those legs…

Still furious about witnessing her first love get shot by her father, 15-year-old Angel felt vengeful. Enclosed in her bathroom between her toilet and her shower, she was unemotional and amazed that she didn't go looney on Wiley after he pulled his trigger. She didn't have time to be emotional when she had to devise a plan compliments of being a witness, and there was no way she was going to let her father get away with bodily harm. Specially not on the strength that the only man that ever loved her became a target on her behalf. Wiley may have threatened Terrace not to go to the authorities, but the person he really should've been threatening was Angel.

Not wanting to see his yucky

daughter's nudeness, Wiley ended up putting Angel's tantalizing gateway back on its hinges, but he should've left it off so he could've monitored America's Next Top porn star also known as Angel. Knowing Angel that little slut would probably nail a sheet up for a door. Nobody could stop her not even a roadblock.

After taking a hot shower, Angel got dressed, changed her sexy sheets and comforter on her bed, and called her boo Terrace to check up on him before she set her plan in motion.

"Are you okay bay?" Angel asked Terrace when he answered the phone after the first ring.

"Yeah I'm okay. I still can't believe your pops really shot me. And on top of that your pops made me jump out of a moving vehicle so now I got a bullet wound, some

137

scrapes and some bruises, and I still got to deal with him. What the hell is he going to do next Angel?

"You talking like you're going to let Wiley Wild scare you away or something?"

"Angel what is up with you calling your pops by his first name? Don't you think that's disrespectful?"

"Does that hurt your feelings or something because it's nothing you can do to fix that? That's between me and Wiley."

"I don't got time to argue with you. I'm going to be at the hospital for a couple of days, and I feel better now that they removed the bullet out of my arm. You know those doctors were asking me a billion questions, but I didn't say anything."

"Don't worry baby you don't have to. I

promise you I'm going to take care of everything."

"Angel please don't make this your fight." Terrace's words went through one of Angel's ears and out the other.

"I love you bay, but I got to go."

Soon as Angel pressed the end call function on her cell phone, she called her a yellow cab and made her way to a place where she was going to get redemption.

Poor Angel had malice for her father and annoyance towards her mother for dropping her off at her father's house. Angel didn't understand why her mother couldn't send her somewhere else while she went overseas. Nydia needed a huge relief from her daughter's wild and outrageously disappointing conduct. No matter what, Nydia would always have unconditional love for her daughter, and would never judge her, but damn Angel something had to give. How much teenage bullshit can a thoroughbred mother take?

Angel begged her mother to let her go elsewhere, but Nydia refused because she didn't trust her child with just anybody. Nydia was hoping by her leaving Angel with her father that they could improve their father/daughter bond and hoping was all she was going to be able to do. Nydia also hoped that finally Wiley would act like a concerned father who actually cared about his daughter.

Nydia despised Angel's boyfriend Terrace. She thought just maybe Terrace would be afraid to try some slick shit with Angel over her father's house especially since he knew that he was a police authority, but knowing that just made Terrace more tempted to be with his precious angel in disguise.

Somehow, someway Nydia had to escape the mid-life dilemmas she was experiencing from her home life. She was a workaholic, she had a wild teenager, she felt like a single parent, and she was dealing with other inner battles. Nydia was aging quickly and she was becoming very ill, because it seemed like the spirit of extramarital sex had taken her daughter captive and was not going to let her go until somebody in her life casted it out.

Three days straight at work, Nydia fainted and was sent home and to the hospital for evaluation and observation. Lucky for her she didn't slip up under their microscope and she fainted each time into someone's arms. Once her corporate job got word of Nydia's jaw dropping results of her stress test, her blood pressure, and her high-risk EKG results, it was a wrap. Nydia would be likely to have a stroke or heart attack if she didn't take off for a while. They were happy to personally handpick their favorite employee Nydia a 30 day getaway vacation out of the country especially since the staff at Nydia's job valued her employment. They knew there was something troubling her in life and she had not taken off work or been late to work in a year tops.

Nydia's job was going to make Wiley look after Angel even if he refused. They knew Nydia would leave in a heartbeat even if it meant she was temporarily separated from Angel. Nydia had to regain her strength and rest her mind.

Unfortunately, Nydia and Wiley were nothing, but another couple who voluntarily let themselves become a statistic of divorce. At the time the two of them had something lacking in their fighting skills and had a flawed definition of love, but the thing that really sank their boat was the fact that they got married for more wrong reasons then right reasons.

All Nydia asked Wiley to do was take care of Angel until her return, and of course as Angel's father he agreed wanting to be closer to his daughter, which was going to be difficult because his daughter didn't want to be close to him. She didn't want to be in the same car as him, she didn't want to be in the same house as him, and she didn't never even want to talk to him on the phone. She never called him, she

143

hadn't seen him in years, and didn't even know why she had her own room at his house because she never went over there to visit him, but Wiley gave her a room anyway hoping one day she would finally come to her senses and forgive him. Basically, she didn't want anything to do with her father. She even wished she had an absent father instead of the father she had.

Long while after Nydia and Wiley divorced, he ended up getting re-engaged to a witch named Delilah. There is nothing wrong with remarriage, but there is something wrong with putting a woman or a man before your child and that is exactly what Wiley did. His new fiancé didn't like Angel, didn't like kids, didn't even have any children, and didn't want any so how did she manage to marry Wiley knowing he had a daughter? She pretended to like Angel in the beginning and bond with her until one day she finally cracked.

Wiley begged his second fiancé Delilah to take Angel to Somerset Mall with her to do some last minute shopping for their honeymoon and after a lot of begging she agreed. Delilah wasn't even paying any attention to Angel at the mall; she was just going about her business like Angel wasn't even there. Consequently, Delilah lost Angel in the mall and she just shrugged her shoulders and kept on shopping until she dropped. Luckily, Angel had a cell phone and called her daddy. Of course he was upset and immediately called Delilah, and made her stop her black card flow to meet Angel somewhere, which really ticked her off so when she finally caught up with Angel she was the most bewitched woman ever.

All Angel did was ask her soon-to-be stepmother could they stop and get something to eat and that's when Delilah snapped.

"Look you little pigeon-toed wench if you want something to eat wait to you get home because we're not stopping. You already prolonged me enough today. You then snitched on me to your daddy and got him blowing up my phone looking for your Raggedy Ann ass. You should've been following me more closely. It ain't my fault your parents didn't put your ass in a charter school."

"You're not my mother. I don't need a charter school to know that's not how you talk to anybody's child. If you don't get me something to eat I'm going to call my daddy again."

"We'll see about that," Delilah claimed as she snatched Angel's little cute purse out her hand, dug her phone out, dropped it, and broke it into a trillion pieces.

"You see your broke ass, stone age phone? Now shut your winy ass up and come on."

"Your evil and you're going to pay for that."

"Call me what you want, but I don't like you never did and never will and there's nothing you can do about it. Now spend the rest of this time at the mall with me knowing that." That was the worst trip Angel had ever had to the mall. And when she got home she told her mother everything including how Delilah broke her phone. And Nydia ended up telling

Wiley, but he just shrugged it off and then he married the broad. And after they got married, Delilah kept Wiley away from Angel as much as she could. Even for the annual daddy/daughter dance that meant the world to Angel every single year, for ten years, until her so called daddy stood her up. Angel blamed Delilah and resented Wiley like she had never resented anybody before. All because Wiley put a woman before his child and missed an important father/daughter milestone. Once he realized he married the wrong woman it was too late because his daughter was already screwed up in the head.

Just as Wiley promised he was going to deal with his little "angel" even though there was nothing angelic about Angel anymore he was surprised once again by the little freak of nature he created.

Wiley was expecting to find Angel asleep or marinating on her worst behaviors, but the daddy/daughter shocks for the day were not over because Angel was not in her room alone. Obviously, it meant nothing to her to have gotten caught. She didn't see the bigger picture that she was disrespecting herself, and her father's household, and she was taking advantage of her current living situation with her father. She only saw and felt the current high she was getting off more sex. The only difference was a different partner and this time this sexual partner might land Wiley in a prison cell.

This time it wasn't no moaning in the air, but there was an eerie feeling in the atmosphere. When Wiley reached Angel's

149

room and opened her door once again he tried to forget about his previous memoirs from earlier. Wiley couldn't grasp what was going on inside of his daughter's ill head. After getting a full glimpse of the scene he knew his daughter needed psychological help. She didn't need a brief talk, a punishment, or a phone call to Nydia. She needed REAL HELP because obviously Nydia wasn't helping her.

This time around Angel was all roughed up in the heat of aggression. She had contusions scattered vertically and horizontally across her body. Her wrists and her ankles were tied to her bedposts like she wanted to be confined. She was so out of it she didn't even have a clue Wiley was in the room nor did her current partner. She was spread out on her bed, flat on her stomach where her partner was administering his ferocity from behind. Studying the male that was knocking the bottom out of Angel's walls, Wiley felt a connection to him, and then it dawned on him that he had been betrayed.

"Eon, what the fuck are you doing here? So you're fucking my daughter too? Damn who isn't fucking my daughter?" Wiley asked the world wondering if the whole world was or already had fucked his daughter too.

"What does it look like he's doing here Wiley? He certainly didn't come here to visit you," Angel declared.

"And Angel I see you still haven't learned your lesson. So you went and found you somebody at my job to fuck as if fucking your boyfriend wasn't enough. At the rate your going by the time your 16 you're not even

151

going to have a pussy down there. Hey, Eon did you know she just got finished fucking a couple hours ago? How does that feel to know that you didn't hit it first?"

"Fuck you and your opinion Wiley! That's the only thing you can do is insult me. Why don't you stop waltzing up in my room like we cool or something. I don't need you to check on me, I don't like you, and I don't understand why you want just get the fuck on and go do your job. Maybe you don't like coming, but I do so leave!"

"I'm not leaving shit, not without Eon. I know you better not step foot in the Clinton Township Police Department ever again in your pitiful life. You will never be a cop in this town. I promise you that rookie."   "Whoa, whoa, whoa, not so fast chief," Eon shook his deviant little head.

"You will never be a cop in this town once Angel, Terrace, and I get finished with your ass. You dirty cop, shooting innocent people with your gun, non-protective joke. Are you going to shoot me too because unlike Terrace I shoot back? And even if I don't hit you with a bullet today, I will or I will get somebody else to do it for me."

"Are you trying to coerce a cop?"

"No what I'm telling you is that you need to mind your business while I finish my nut. I'm going to finish what I started, and you're going to go back to work or do whatever you do in your spare time. And then when I'm done you can talk to Angel."

Wiley felt like a board between a hammer and a nail. On one hand, he could bury

Eon, but then that would be a dead body on his record, and on the other hand, he could shoot him away also, but Eon was liable to snitch, and Angel and Eon were already conspiring against him so what could he do besides leave his house as he was told by two houseguests.

Wiley Woodward was acting like he was born with a dick with no balls. You got enough balls to solve crimes, but you don't have enough balls to fix your family issues? How in the hell was Wiley going to let his slutty daughter and his trainee punk him out? Whether he was going to jail or not he should've killed Eon on GP and he should've killed Angel with him for defying him the way that she was. No matter what Wiley did to Angel in their past, he didn't deserve to feel so powerless by two people he use to respect.

Especially not the last two people on the planet
he ever thought would black-mail him.

In Wiley's brain Angel was beginning
to act like the seed of Chucky and it was about
time he did something deranged so he
pretended to leave Eon and Angel alone as they
continued to engage in their sexual gruesome
acts of nature.

Angrily, Wiley stormed into his garage
desperate for something he could use to
frighten both Angel and Eon. Evidently, Wiley
wasn't individually intimidating enough.
Flipping and skimming through his power
tools he couldn't seem to find the perfect,
ferocious tool yet. Pacing through the garage, a
bright light in his head was beaming on his
chainsaw. Chainsaw was the winner. Wiley
yanked the chainsaw back two times before he

got it running frequently. Trailing in the house Wiley made his way to Angel's sex room. Once again Angel was too enriched in her fuckish ways to peep her crazed daddy. Wiley took his chainsaw and started sawing a large hole in Angel's bedroom wall. Once Wiley completed his hole in the wall, he climbed through his hole, walked over to Angel's bed and began sawing her bed in half.

Angel and Eon rushed into a corner hoping and praying that they were in a median of safety.

"Wiley what the fuck are you doing to my room?" Angel yelled astonished over his chainsaw roars, but he ignored her. Wiley headed for Eon as if he was about to saw him in half next if he didn't get the hell up out of his house. Wiley held his chainsaw high in the air, and yakked his chainsaw chain, and made eye contact with Eon.

Eon still didn't finish his nut, but Wiley won this battle. It was not that deep for Eon to lose his life over a piece of pussy. His life was far too valuable than that.

Eon left his clothes and broke wind to his car. He ran into the neighbor's garbage can trying to pull off from in front of Wiley's hellhole. And after this event he was probably never going to fuck with a police's daughter again. And without a doubt, Wiley probably wasn't ever going to catch Eon fucking with Angel ever, ever, ever again.

Chapter 11: Rebellious Cravings

Who or what can I run to?

Being sober was like surfing on a huge wave and nearly drowning for poor Chisel who was mentally trapped over Haze's place, but Chisel was only trapped over her house because he wanted to be. As many hotels and motels that were waiting to be charged to his black debit card, he could've checked into anyone of them, but he didn't. And if Chisel really felt strongly about staying the hell away from his opprobrious wife, then he would've gone to a homeless shelter.

Mo should've been smarter than the rest of Chisel's flunkies, but she was just as dumb as a high school dropout because she still tolerated his imprudence. She should've known better to share dick with an outlandish bitch.

Chisel's body was craving for that liquid sensation once again, but after he reassessed and rehashed his drinking conditions, he realized there was no point of drinking because no matter how many drinks you consume, the storm is never over. Reflecting on the fire, he theorized he didn't have any enemies, but everyone has secrets and silent enemies. Chisel even found himself thinking about Mo even though he was shacking up at his wife's house. I don't know how any married man can displace himself to think about another woman. Not only that, but getting a divorce, and going to get a divorce are two different things because a man who is getting a divorce means he's already enrolled in the divorce process and is 5 steps away from actually being divorced, and going to get a divorce means he is still 20 steps away from the entire process and has a long way to go. In reality all Chisel had done was tell Haze that he wanted them to separate. Truthfully, he was seeing other people before their separation and there was no validating his actions.

The, "I know you want some and I want some too," smutty look that Chisel and Haze both made Haze wanna stay at home and keep an eye on Chisel especially since he couldn't go far. It was her job to get her man back and knock him down whenever he tried to get away from her so he would always be right by her side.

Chisel had apartment guides and a bunch of daily newspapers spread out on her coffee table directly open to the real estate sections. Chisel had already called a few numbers that were listed, but he was still indecisive. Numerous properties were highlighted and crossed-out like words in a crossword puzzle. He had a bunch of different housing prospects, but Haze wasn't having it.

You ain't going nowhere baby not on my watch. You should've been smart enough to marry somebody else, but you married me now you have to deal with the consequences. And you should've cleaned your mess up, and maybe it wouldn't have gotten thrown away.

Once Chisel fell asleep she purposely threw all of his moving resources away. Apartment guides were free and newspapers were just 99 cents so it wasn't like Haze really did some major life unjustness to Chisel. Apparently, Chisel was never going to get anything accomplished with his hating ass wife around.

When Chisel woke up he noticed that the coffee table was squeaky clean. It didn't have not one dish, one wet mark, or one paper on it which was fine, but once Chisel looked around and remembered where he was he knew he had to get his own again because him and Haze just didn't mix and he needed his independence back.

"What did you do with my shit Haze?"

"What shit are you talking about?" Haze looked dumbfounded, even though she wasn't playing.

"Bitch you know I had all kinds of moving leads laying all over the coffee table!"

"Oh you were still using that? I was just trying to clean up for you and I thought you were done with that stuff so I threw it away."

"There you go. You knew I wasn't done with that shit, but you threw it away anyway. Don't try to sugar coat it. If you gon do something shady at least you can be a woman about it, but I guess that's too much to ask for seeing that you still act like a little girl." Unlike Chisel, Haze loved to argue and seeing as though she was losing, she had to turn the tables on Chisel and spark up another subject matter.

"I bet you don't talk to Mimosa like this so why do you treat that hot yellow bitch better then you treat me?"

"This is not about how I talk to Mimosa and how I talk to Mimosa is none of your business. I wish you acted like her and maybe we wouldn't be getting a divorce."

"I don't want to be Mimosa and if we were getting a divorce why are you here? How about you show me some divorce papers so I can sign them? That's exactly what I thought you don't have any. And probably haven't even called one lawyer about a divorce yet, but you want to be separated. I don't know why because you do what you do and I do what I do regardless so stop acting brand new." Chisel and Haze would've probably still been going at it if his phone didn't start ringing.

"Don't tell me you're going to answer that right now?" Chisel hand-motioned for Haze to go upstairs somewhere and find herself some business.

"Bitch be quiet our conversation can wait a minute. Why don't you go find yourself upstairs and I'll be up there when I'm done."

164

"Hello."

"Chisel shit just got real," Gregory complained sounding like his life had just got struck by 10 lightning bolts.

"I'm sure nothing can be worse than temporarily cohabitating with your ex-wife and being homeless, but it probably is so what happened?"

"It's all over the news Chisel. My girlfriend's pretty face is all over the local news. Today authorities found Rosario and her cousin Chiquita in the trunk of a black 2013 Impala SS sitting in a vacant field in between two burnt down houses. And nobody can't tell me nothing. How is it that the Oakland County medical examiner can't tell me nothing and they get paid to analyze bodies every day?" Chisel was speechless and motionless and even though Rosario was still an evil bitch in his mind, he felt she didn't deserve to die. Chisel had never heard his best friend sound so hurt and alone before in none of their years of friendship, and he never heard his friend cry a snot-nosed cry before either.

"I'm sorry for your loss bro. I know how much you loved and cared about Rosario."

"Somebody killed my baby man, Rosario was my baby. I wanted to spend the rest of my life with that girl. I told her to stop hanging around Chiquita, but she didn't want to listen. I knew that girl was trouble."

"If there is anything I can do just let me know bro."

"Maybe you can talk to Haze for me and see if she knows anybody that knows

Chiquita so I can find out why and how this happened. Everybody knows hookers are the best dirt-finders. They can find out anything."

"I hate talking to that bitch, but since this matter is above me, I'll tell her to find out what she can."

"Cool." After Greg confided into Chisel, Chisel couldn't help but reflect on how a person can be here one minute and gone the next minute.

*****

When Angel's cab arrived at 615 W. Lafayette Blvd, she couldn't wait to pitch her front page story. Ears were going to be fastening, computer keys were going to be typing, and pens were going to be writing, because she had a story that no Detroit journalist would deny. There was something

167

biologically wrong with men of the law and she was going to prove it.

As Angel walked into the Detroit Free Press headquarters, she stopped at the receptionist desk to find out exactly where she needed to go.

"Yes, I'm here to pitch a story to a journalist on staff, where do I need to go? Who can I talk to?"

"Shouldn't you be in a school somewhere young lady?" The female receptionist determined by Angel's appearance not used to seeing teenagers come into the office to pitch stories.

"I would've been in school if my daddy didn't shoot my boyfriend in front of my very eyes. My daddy serves on the Clinton Township force so why do cops shoot innocent people and think they can get away it? I had to come somewhere where I knew people wouldn't turn me away."

"I see where this is going and the Detroit Free Press would definitely be interested in an article like this so I'm going to get a journalist right away for you. Just take a seat in the lobby for me sweetie. I promise it won't be long."

Columnists loved writing articles about corrupt city cops, so when Gail, the newest addition to the press heard that she was going to be interviewing a young woman about witnessing a crime of a public figure, she was amped. She was about to have a fat incentive from this cover story and she was going to have major credentials with this incredible article in her journalism portfolio.

169

Gail walked out and basically ambushed Angel herself so she could make sure Angel was as complaisant as possible. She gave Angel ever humanly gesture of conformity that she possibly could for the time being.

"So Angel what brings you here today?"

"My daddy is a cop and I witnessed him shoot my boyfriend in the shoulder. My boyfriend Terrace Smith is still recovering at Henry Ford Macomb Hospital and my daddy Wiley Woodward, the police chief of the Clinton Township Police Department is the perp. Granted my boyfriend and I were just finishing up a school science project on gravity, and I know I'm not supposed to have visitors in the house without my daddy's consent, my daddy totally overacted in this situation. My boyfriend was scared for his dear life. He was begging my daddy for his mercy, but it was like my daddy was listening to voices in his head because he was irresponsive. My boyfriend was only trying to leave without being harmed or causing harm, but my daddy held him at gunpoint and shot him. He's been acting real crazy lately. I really do think he needs to be evaluated for PTSD (post traumatic stress disorder). My boyfriend didn't want me to come forward, but I'm doing this for society because there is too much unreported violence going on in our community today, and much of that violence is being done by people who think that they are above the law. You give a man a badge and he thinks he's superhuman."

"Wow Angel you really took my breath away. You really do have a heart-breaking story and you seem like a very inquisitive young lady. I'm really sorry that you had to experience this."

"No teenager should have to witness such a thing at 15-years-old. The bad apart about this is I feel like this is my entire fault. If I wouldn't have invited Terrace over without my father's consent then he wouldn't be in this impaired predicament. If I didn't find myself skipping school trying to finish a school assignment then maybe I wouldn't be sitting here. I was just being a typical teenager who was actually ditching school for an educational purpose. My daddy might be a cop, but our father/daughter bond has been flawed for years and now I just feel that it's time to let the cat out of the hat. How many more times is he and other cops going to get away with these types of crimes?" Angel made herself burst out into fake crocodile tears and Gail handed Angel a box of tissue.

"Your totally right Angel, I'm going to make sure this story hits the stand tomorrow. I'm just going to have to ask you a few more questions to make sure I covered everything. I just need to make sure that this is what you really want to do because once I print this story I can't undo it. You're going to be stuck with the reality of this tragedy. Your life is going to turn into a circus with cameras, reporters, and angry citizens everywhere you go and I mean everywhere you go practically every time you blink. I'm sure you and your father will never have a relationship again and he's going to write you off out of his life like taxes and you're going to have to relocate everything about your life. You're going to have to testify against your father and you can even file for a lawsuit on the Clinton Township PD if you really feeling bossy.

"This is exactly what I want to do and I don't nor will I ever have any regrets about it."

"I don't even see how you can look at your dad let alone sleep in the same house with him after that?"

"I really don't have anywhere else to go and I don't want to be out on the street. I know what the streets can do to a girl like me."

"I'm sure you need a ride and I wouldn't feel right if I took you back to your father's place so are you sure there isn't anywhere else I can take you?"

Angel didn't put any thought into where she would go after she exposed her father, but Gail was making a whole lot of sense so she began to formulate a quick plan of action in her head. She definitely needed money and a little overnight bag, and she could go sit by Terrace's bedside until he was released from the hospital and then runoff into no man's land with him so that's exactly what she was going to do. Everything was working out for Angel like everything she was doing was destined to happen.

If it was one thing that Angel knew, she knew how to use her words wisely because words start wars. She was absolutely in the premature stages of starting a war with her family and the law because she was going to persecute her father to her utmost degree.

Chapter 12: Pain or Pleasure

Black is a painful color....

In Mimosa's neighborhood, birds were chirping and new businesses were flourishing in popularity and productivity. Siege Piercings was the first and only Detroit based piercing shop to come to Michigan on the Eastside of Detroit. Strictly specializing in a wide array of body piercings, they were staffed with the coldest piercers in the city.

Siege Piercings was snatching all of the local tattoo shops piercing customers' from up under their piercing skins and giving them better quality, faster service, numerous piercing styles, and a staff full of piercers.

back in July 2012

When Siege Piercings had their grand opening they were advertising buy one piercing get one piercing free all day and all night. It was like a class reunion merged with a family reunion until the corner turned into a crime scene. There was no way you could stand in that hot, jagged line without seeing somebody familiar. Once an irate, identifiable gunman who didn't have any type of disguise over his face came blasting up the piercing extravaganza with his flying gunshots; once free spirits started becoming victims, once sirens started roaring through the heavens, and police made Siege Piercings shutdown, all the fun was over.

A few weeks later when Siege Piercings was off the radar, Mimosa began a newfound friendship with one of the piercers in the shop who went by the name of Sebastian. Sebastian insured her of free piercings long as she let him suck her nectar, open up her treasure chest with his joystick or both after his shift was over. Never did Sebastian feel like he was being used by a gold-digger, even though most of the time Mo shot him down with a period lie. I don't understand how or why she would give her juice box up for a piercing when she could just work hard like other hardworking citizens, save her money, and cash herself out on her wants and needs. The disgrace that Mo was taking just to get a damn piercing would live with her forever, and if she was supposed to be all for Chisel, why did she still have wondering eyes for so many other men?

Already Mimosa had 10 bodily piercings, but once you get one piercing, you can't stop, you have to get more. All Mo could think about was when Chisel told her how much he would love her if she got her clitoris pierced. Mo heard that clitoris piercings were extremely sexually stimulating when subjected to gentle manipulation or vibration and that was right up her sleazy alley. Mo wanted an unthinkable piercing and she wanted to surprise Chisel with something unforgettable since her competition was steep. Mo was ready to carry out her most painful and dangerous piercing yet.

Cooling out in the piercing lobby, Mo was waiting for Sebastian to call her back to his private booth when she saw some strange girl who immediately reminded her of Chisel. After overhearing a short chat Mo was having with another girl about piercings, the strange girl immediately started chatting with Mo. This girl had sunglasses on inside a piercing shop like it was summertime when it was like an icicle outside on a cloudy day. *Who wears sunglasses indoors? I guess girls like this girl do. She must've been hiding something, but if that was so why was she even parading around in public if she knew how much attention her non-matching stunna shades could get her?*

"You mind if I ask you a question," the girl asked Mo who really didn't need her permission to ask her anything and was going to ask Mo whatever she wanted to whether she said yes or no.

"Go ahead."

"Why do you want to get your clit pierced? Is it for pain or for pleasure?" Mo didn't see any point in sugarcoating the truth about her piercing so she decided to put the nosy girl out her curiosity.

"My relationship is complicated, but my guy always wanted me to get my clit pierced so here I am."

"You girls just don't learn." Just as the girl was saying that she dropped her phone on the floor and bended down to pick it up. She was trying to hurry up and fetch her loose sunglasses that just swung off her face which revealed her atrocious, black eye.

"What's that supposed to mean?"

"I'm surprise you don't recognize me. I've seen you around Chisel before. I'm his little sister Chenille." Mo grimed Chenille up and down to try to open her senses and when she remembered exactly who Chenille was she was still a stranger to her."

"I can't believe your actually about to

get your clit pierced for him. Do you really think that's going to make him want you more? Don't you know he's married and probably ain't never going to get a divorce? Don't you know he's a player and probably got a whole train of girls who probably already been here done that? Don't you know every time after he leaves you, gives you a little kiss on your rosy cheeks or whatever he does before he goes he's running right back to his wife?"

"That's your opinion of the situation, but not mine and for the record you don't have any room to give anybody advice by the looks of your eye, you obviously don't get it. If I had a black eye I wouldn't be sitting up at no damn piercing parlor trying to get a piercing. I would be sitting at a police station filing a police report, calling cousin Pookie and them to come get me and my things. I would be sitting somewhere safe re-evaluating my relationship and waiting on my eye to heal."

"Maybe so, but today is my birthday, and I'm not going to let this black eye stop me from celebrating it the way I want to black eye or no black eye. And why you talking I'm surprised I ain't seen you with no purple-black eyes or busted up lips yet or maybe I just ain't seen you with one yet because you was too busy hiding behind closed doors so nobody would know. Yet again I know my brother and I know how he is with a light skinned girl. He just doesn't trust them," Mo sneered at Chenille.

"For the record your brother never put his hands on me and never will. And another thing I really don't think you know your

184

brother like you think you do so please do me a favor and don't say anything else to me about him. Sister or no sister if you keep talking to me sideways you not going to be nobody's sister. I will finish whoever blacked your eye job's and black the other one and then you'll have to super glue them glasses to your sideburns so they want fall off. And I still can't believe you let somebody black your eye on your birthday. I guess he gave your eye birthday licks huh." The subject matter really wasn't funny, but Mo didn't need anybody coaching her about Chisel especially not his beat up little sister so she said what she had to say. Lucky for Chenille, Sebastian saved her black-eyed day because it was about to be a catfight and all the Siege employees were going to put their poker chips on Mimosa.

When Mo entered Sebastian's private room she gave him a wet kiss on the lips. A kiss on the lips was a bit much for just a piercer.

"Aw shit I'm getting kisses today and to what do I owe this honor?"

"You just so good to me and I thought I would give you a kiss."

"How sweet is that so what are we getting pierced today?"

"I want you to pierce my clit."

"Did you just say what I thought you just said? I really don't think I heard you correctly. Can you run that by me again?" Sebastian couldn't believe his filthy ears.

Even though Sebastian was another man who should've been off limits to her he wasn't. Sebastian had a girl and a kid and still made it his job to push up on Mo so hard you would've thought that he had been a single man forever. After their kiss, Sebastian and Mo talked a little bit while he got his equipment ready for Mo's piercing of the day. And just like always he did his job perfectly and once he got off of work, Mo was going to have to do hers.

■■■■■■■■■■■■■■■■■■■■■■■■■■■■■■■■■■■■■ı

Chapter 13: Nose Candy

Cocaine is a hell of a drug…

The customer of the day was one of Haze's eastside regulars named Lorenz. Lorenz had that Arab money and probably could fuck every girl in the world, but like Haze and her hustle he liked having specific regulars too. He had a chef, trick, maid, girlfriend, butler, manager, publicist, stylist and etc and everybody had better play their cards right or else they could consider themselves permanently terminated from his enterprises.

Lorenz was finger engaged to be married to his girlfriend Queenly on Valentine's Day of February 14, 2013 so why would an engaged man be committing pre-infidelity acts already before he could even tie the knot? Simply because Queenly put the capital "V" in virgin and she stood strong to withholding her womanhood no matter how many times Lorenz tried to let Queenly make her cherry blossom. There was no way in hell Queenly was going to give up her VV until Lorenz walked her down the aisle and married her. Wedding rings, marriage license, honey moon, wedding pictures, Lorenz's last name, all that shit had to be in place first and foremost. Unlike most females her age, she wasn't going to be a part of the baby momma statistics who ended up with babies without baby daddies.

Selfishly, Lorenz found himself a special trick who became Haze and he paid her well to fill and refill his sexual urges. The day of Lorenz bachelor party was going to be the last time that he smashed Haze. After that her

189

ass was going to be grass because he planned to finally be loyal to his wife-to-be after he tied the knot. Since when did a bitch have to give up some pussy for a man to be faithful?

Just when Haze and Lorenz were about to get it in, Lorenz stopped her in her undressing tracks, unbuttons, unbuckles, and unsnaps. She was just about to unsnap her bra and slide out her matching g-string when he interrupted.

"I don't need you to get naked this time. You can take off your bra, but leave your g-string on," Lorenz confused his trick because there was not one single lick or fuck that he didn't want to see Haze butt booty naked.

"What do you mean? I thought you wanted the usual?"

"I heard some things about your boy

lately, I mean your husband and I don't think me and you should get done like that anymore. As far as the head goes, I would never ever give that up because your head game is too cold so cold that I think I might have to pay you to teach my fiancé lessons."

"What exactly did you hear and what does that got to do with me and you? You know how I do. I stay at the clinic getting check-ups, I stay at the drug store buying condoms, and Mirena is my best friend so what is the problem because I know your relationship don't have you tripping on me?"

"This doesn't have anything to do with my relationship so watch your slutty mouth! You know better to speak about her in my presence. She not planting no types of bug in my ear. The streets are talking and as much as

191

you be in them I'm surprised that you haven't heard."

"What do I need to hear? You treating me like I got something dude?"

"Let's just say your man got you looking real stupid out here."

"Are you trying to say my husband is cheating on me?"

"In so many words, yes he is. He's cheating on you with Cocaine."

"Who the fuck is Cocaine?"

"It's certainly not a bitch. I'm talking about the drug."

"You must have him mixed him up with somebody else who might resemble him. And what does his supposed cocaine habit got to do with us living it up?"

"Nope I know for a fact it's your

husband and it has everything to do with us now because people will do anything for cocaine and when I say anything I mean anything and I don't trust that."

"And I don't trust you," so Haze put her clothes back on and left as quickly as she came. She hopped in her car and began driving to her house to confront Chisel. And on the way there she had to call her good friend to see if she was already hip to Chisel's new addiction. She knew practically everything that went down in the street or was going to go down in the streets including who, what, where, and why. She was a nosy bitch who had the 411 on everything.

(Ring, Ring).

"I miss you girl where you been?" Kindle answered.

"Kindle I miss you too, but I have to

ask you a serious question and don't lie to me either." Kindle was beginning to dread where this appalling conversation was headed.

"You can ask me anything Haze you know I don't sugarcoat anything not even for your sensitive ears."

"Is Chisel on crack?" And there it goes that one thing that Kindle was keeping a deep, dark secret. That one thing that Kindle wanted Haze to find out on her own without Kindle's assistance. And now she had to confirm it or else she was going to have to deal with Haze's ire when she gutted her ass for withholding information.

"I'm sorry Haze he is," Kindle cried empathetically.

"What were you waiting for to tell me? Until I told you I got AIDS/HIV from his ass?

Until he burnt down my house and robbed me dry?"

"Thanks for nothing bitch," Haze hung up even more livid then what she was prior to calling Kindle. Everybody knew the dirty truth except for her. There was no way in hell Haze was going to let Chisel get away with this atrocity.

***

Chisel was starting to become real nostalgic sitting alone in between Haze's four walls. He was now ready to get to the bottom of who, what, and why his house was set on fire so he got dressed and ready to take his narrow ass down to the police station to give his official statement. Police stations made Chisel sweat and itch especially since he was a convicted felon/ex basketball player, and probably had some warrants out for his arrest, but this was something that he just had to suck up and do. Anything beats being under Haze's black angel wings.

Chisel took a deep breath and then he walked in to the same station that his ex-girlfriend Cyn walked in.

"Yes, I'm here to give my statement," Chisel told a deputy on staff.

"What's your name sir?"

"My name is Chisel Simmons."

"Yes Chief Wiley Woodward is on your case. I'll let him know that you're here and he'll be with you shortly so just have a seat in the lobby."

Chief Wiley Woodward. I guess I'm about to be singing like a canary with a department head which beats speaking with a police rookie. I know this shit better not take

forever, and I know this damn detective better

have some answers for me because I need to

know exactly what happened on the morning of

September 25, 2012 and why. The police chief

has had enough free time to do his forensic and

analytical bullshit thoroughly and figure it out

so he better not be trying to flip this shit on me

because I wouldn't do no dumb ass shit like

that to myself especially not at a time like this

when I was living good.

"Chisel Simmons," a strong, stern

voice called out from the back.

"I'm Chisel Simmons," Chisel got up

and followed Mr. Woodward as he led the way.

"What took you so long to come in here

man? If I had a house like yours and it caught

on fire out of the blue, I would've had my ass at

the police station the same day and every day after that until somebody told me something I could live with."

"Well life knows how to slow you down bro."

"I hear that," so Chisel took a seat as Mr. Woodward seated himself and prepared himself for further questioning.

"I'm not going to beat around the bush so where were you on the morning of September 25, 2013?"

"I was in Detroit with a hangover sleeping in my car because my wife and I were arguing so I made myself leave."

"Why would you leave your own house? Why wouldn't you just tell your wife to go home especially if y'all are separated?"

"I was probably drunk and I am my

own worst enemy especially when I'm drunk. I do and say crazy things when I'm drunk, but never would I have done nothing like this."

"How do you know that you didn't set this fire on a drunken rampage?"

"That house cost me a good grip. I wanted my grandkids to die in that house and I don't even have grandkids yet. Has anyone else came in here and made any statements because the person you need to be questioning isn't me?"

"Well sir, I'm really not supposed to talk about my witnesses, but I need to ask you some questions pertaining to one of the witnesses on this case. Who is Cyn Clarkson?" Chisel couldn't believe his crazy ex-girlfriend was correlated in all of this lunacy. *How in the fuck does she know about any of this shit? That bitch lives in Detroit so why in the fuck would*

she be snooping around my house? I haven't

seen my son that I have with her in a few weeks,

but I haven't spoken to her on some real shit in

months. I thought that bitch evaporated to

another state or something.

"You have to be kidding man that's my
ex-girlfriend slash baby mother. What the fuck
does she know about this fire or does she say
she know about this fire? My baby mother is a
cynical liar."

"Tell me a brief description of y'all
relationship."

"I ended the relationship because she
caught me cheating and I woke up to staring in
the barrel of her gun. Instead of winding up in
the paper as an article, I ended the relationship.
We have a son together that she will not let me

200

see. When I get back up on my feet I plan on taking her ass to the Friend of the Court and establishing some type of shared custody."

"She expressed no ill-favor towards you at all and she is determined that your wife did it. She gave me lots of evidence to back-up her determination. "

"I'm not going to lie Haze has a lot of hostility towards me. Therefore the motive is definitely relevant, so I cannot even say that Cyn is lying about this. She might actually be on to something."

"What we need to do now is get Haze up in here so we can hear her side of the story. I need her contact information right away or should I do a pop-up visit at her house? I want to make sure she's not going to flee before we can close this case. I don't have all year to spend on one case. I got a shit load of cases to solve and trust me the cases that I have are far more paramount then this simple-minded case here."

"I just want to know who did this to me and why and I want them to suffer the way that I'm suffering right now being homeless. Living with a woman that you are no longer in love with is for the birds."

"I can preclude the results of this case right now, I just have to do my research and question Haze. After that the case will be solved so I'll be in touch. Thank you for coming in today."

Finally, Chisel felt like he had somebody on his skewed sides as it pertained to the law and justice. What goes around comes around like a hula hoop so either karma was a beautiful bitch or Chisel's sinuous ways were finally catching up to him.

***

Angel was pleased that Gail bargained to be her chauffeur until Angel finally got to her final destination so Angel's first requested stop was Wiley's house. Thankfully, Wiley wasn't home, and Angel wanted to beat him home so she ran into the house as swiftly as she could. She rummaged through her drawers and stuffed a few items into her backpack, and went into the kitchen where she stole Wiley's spare credit card from up under the Kool-Aid canister and put it in her pocket. Then she got back in the car, threw her seatbelt back on, and rode off to her next stop with Gail.

"Is everything okay Angel?" Gail wondered as she noticed Angel's low, depressed posture in the seat.

"Everything is fine. We need to stop at the nearest Bank of America next. I need to withdraw some money out of my account for expenses." It didn't even register to Gail to question a 15-year-old having a bank account, but elite parents often handicapped their children with bank accounts so it wasn't really unordinary.

Gail pulled over at the next Bank of America she saw so Angel could withdraw some fast cash from the ATM. The magic pin code was 6934, she hit checking account, and the ATM dispensed 40 crisp bills. ATM limits were a bitch, but there was always going to be tomorrow. Angel snatched the money and secured it in her Coach wallet, balled up her transaction receipt, and threw it into the parking lot garbage on her way back in Gail's

ride and headed straight for Terrace. She hoped

her and Terrace could be the happy couple that

they were destined to be and runoff into the

moonlight, but there was no such thing as a

happy couple.

Chapter 14: Off the Wall

Deal with It…

Nydia finally returned home from her wonderful expense-paid vacation in Berlin, Germany. She had enough deep breathes and fresh uncontaminated air to regenerate her inner strength. Her mother intuition was finally kicking back in her soft and sensitive skull. "If I brought her into this world, I can take her out of this world," Nydia kept telling herself.

Why Angel's parents acted like they were so afraid of her was puzzling because Angel was just a 15-year-old freak who you could pop like a cherry. How in the hell was she ever going to harm her parents when all she ever wanted to do was cock her fast legs open and take some dick.

Wiley was told not to burden Nydia during her time of mental incarceration so Angel's mother was completely uninformed about any of the mortifying events that have been taking place at Wiley's house. All Nydia knew was that she was home and she was going to go get her little Angel, and take her home with her so Nydia called Wiley so he would be aware of everything that was going on.

When Wiley saw that Nydia was calling him, he couldn't wait to enlighten his child's mother about all of Angel's dirt

"Nydia I hope your calling me to tell me that you're back in town?"

"Hey to you to Wiley, how has life been treating you in the past month?"

"Life, what life do I have? My life is over thanks to that little bitch you call a daughter."

"Do not speak of our daughter like that to me."

"You really haven't seen the paper yet have you?"

"What are you talking about Wiley?"

"Go get a paper and call me back when you get one," Wiley commanded and then he hung up not allowing an interjection.

Nydia had one direct goal and that was to pick-up Angel. Where all this bellicosity was coming from was awkward, but since it had to be something big if Wiley was making a big deal out of it she figured she would grab a paper.

Nydia drove to the nearest gas station to grab a newspaper. Before the paper was even paid for her eyes grew immensely large and she almost died reading the sharp headlines in big, bold, black print. "Police Chief is a Bad Father/Sharp Shooter." Nydia began skimming through the article with her eyes reading about how the Clinton Township Police Chief shot his daughter's boyfriend in the midst of studying and basically treats his daughter like a crack head on the street. There was no way in hell Nydia was about to waste her 99 cents on this bullshit.

Nydia had to call Wiley back to find out if any of this headliner bullshit was true.

"So did you read it?" Wiley answered without a friendly greeting.

"I read it is it true?"

"It's true that I shot Angel's boyfriend, but everything else is a lie Angel made up to punish me."

"Where is Angel?"

"I don't know where Angel is and I don't care. She better not ever come back here. She hasn't been back here since she ratted me out to the press. Clearly, she knew better than that."

"How did this even happen?" Nydia was at a loss for words.

"Since you've been gone Angel has been like a fucking machine. Every time I close my eyes and turn my back she is fucking. She's been skipping school and fucking random niggas in my home when I'm gone to work. I've caught two different niggas in my house already one who I knew from work and one who I despise. And yes I shot one with intent to wound not to kill. I mean damn I caught them fucking; what is a father supposed to do when he catches his daughter fucking Dominatrix style. I should be the only person fucking up in here, but I'm not so what have you been teaching our daughter? Are you the one who taught her how to fuck? Did you know that she was even sexually active? Do you condone this shit? And most importantly did you take her to get on birth control so now she thinks having sex is okay?"

"I've been telling you that Angel was out of control and having sex all along, but you wouldn't listen to me remember? Angel is the very reason that I was sick as a dog and my job had to send me away. Why would I teach my daughter how to fuck? What kind of mother do you think I am? How dare you even address me like that? I don't know who you think you're talking too, but were divorced so you better think again. I see all you've been doing is letting my daughter make a fool out of herself instead of protecting her and disciplining her like a father should. You're always so worried about that damn job. That was the only thing you've ever cared about. I mine as well be a single mother because you have never helped me do shit!"

"I did all that I can do for her. I'm wiping my hands clean."

"So you're telling me that you're going to give up on your daughter just like that? You don't have any type of fight in you for her at all?"

"That girl is not my Angel. I don't know who the fuck she is anymore, but I didn't create that, not with my sperm I didn't. Don't bother coming to my house unless you want to be on the local news. I'm sure I'll probably see you again when I'm in court getting locked up for this shit. Thanks a lot for raising a deceptive little bitch," Wiley ended with no resentment for his daughterless declarations.

Fuck Wiley and his 99 problems, all that Nydia cared about now was finding Angel. Nydia wasn't distressed by Angel's behavior at all because she had all the stress she was going to have in her life now it was time to deal. It was time to deal with her ruthless daughter because Nydia was all that Angel really had. And she was going to find her Angel if that was the last thing she did on this Earth.

***

Angel and Gail hugged and said there goodbyes as Gail let Angel out at the Henry Ford Macomb Hospital emergency room entry. Angel got her sticker visitor pass and hopped on the elevator UP to her boo Terrace.

"Hey baby," Angel greeted Terrace with a peck on his drowsy cheeks.

"What's all of this that you have?" Terrace wondered after he noticed Angel's stuffed backpack.

"I'm going to be with you officially starting now."

"Bullshit what did you do Angel?"

"What I did is not important right now, but I can no longer stay at Wiley's house so now you're stuck with me."

"What about your mother? Your mother isn't just going to let us be together either. You know she's going to report your ass missing."

"It doesn't matter all I need is you and all you need is me. You always tell me how you want to leave here, here's our chance. I've got money and I've been looking online, and we can catch the Megabus to a brand new city."

"I've begged you to pack your shit up and leave so many times and you always declined my offer, now all of a suddenly you down for it? What did you do Angel?"

"Terrace let's focus on getting out of here first,
and then I'll tell you what I did."

Terrace knew better to let Angel run game on him, but since he always wanted to skip town with his ghetto princess he was

going to see where time took them. Terrace had

been in the hospital long enough. Now it was

time for him to get medically acquitted. And he

was going to be liberated with his empress

Angel.

Chapter 15: Sleeping With the Enemy

Don't be sorry, be careful....

Nattering was the traditional way to resolve problems, and listening was a conventional method to hear excuses for problems, but Haze wasn't about to do neither. She was burnt out with all of Chisel's indiscretions from his alcoholism, to his disorderly conduct, to his assorted women, to his impiety, and to his infantile mentality, but how could she be so livid when she knew Chisel Simmons better then he knew himself.

If Haze felt Chisel was under-qualified for her love why would she marry him? She was tee'd off because no matter what flaw he had her love for him was impervious, but crack? Finding out the man you love and used to love is on crack is a whole nother story. Finding out your husband, most importantly baby's father finds more pleasure with using street drugs then taking care of his responsibilities is tear-jerking. Crack is the most disgraceful drug in the economy, and it's even more disgraceful when you've slept with a crack feign and didn't even know it.

Crack might be the caviar of street drugs, but when it came to home, crack is an insult. Crack is a powder method of destruction that destroys lives, families, cities, generations, and etc. Crack is demeaning, and crack has no shape or form or business being associated with anything or anyone that has to do with Haze Hilton.

Two people in Haze's inner circle confirmed that she was sleeping with a crack-head so there wasn't any other confirmation she needed. Asking wasn't an option either. She was so inflamed and embittered that Tyler's Perry mad black woman didn't have shit on what she was about to do to Chisel Simmons as a result of the dishonor she felt. Haze's Birchwood liquor cabinet never peered so alluring to her tiger eyes before. Even though drinking was only half of Haze's battles, she could use one of her Korean liquor concoctions right about now.

"Beat him or kill him, beat him or kill him, beat him or kill him?" Haze asked herself over and over again treading her floors until her conscious told her to beat him.

Soon as Chisel turned Haze's spare key in the top lock and was entering her place, Haze was waiting by her front closet like

219

Chisel was a burglar with her metal Louisville Slugger baseball bat in baseball stance ready to strike against Chisel's body. Soon as she had a clear view of him she began hitting him in the head, arms, legs, chest, and back. Everywhere that she could possibly reach.

"Haze it's me what are you doing?" Chisel couldn't understand why his wife was attacking him so violently.

"I know it's you. I'm doing what I should've done a long time ago. I should've been beat the life out of you. Now it's going to take the Jaws of Life to save you after this." Chisel tried to stop Haze, but he kept being overpowered by her deadly, light-headed bat.

"Why are you doing this to me Haze? I know I've fucked up a lot, but damn do we really have to go out like this?"

220

"Shut up, don't speak! I don't want to hear your lies! All you ever did was lie! Crack kills Chisel. Does that ring a fucking bell to you?"

"I'm sorry Haze, I am truly sorry," Chisel stuttered barely able to speak.

"Don't be sorry, be careful. You should've been more careful then to try to shit on a bitch like me. We could've worked it out like we always do, but crack is a no-go. You could've done anything else to me, but to let me find out your doing crack and I'm sleeping with the enemy you have to suffer!" Haze established striking Chisel hit after hit, force after force until Chisel was face down on the ground and was practically unidentifiable.

After Haze saw that she had beaten Chisel unconscious, she wiped her mouth like

Chisel was a piece of filth, threw her bat across the room, patted herself on the back, and called 911.

"9-1-1 how can I help you?"

"Yes my husband is unconscious, and I need an ambulance now on 38010 Club House Lane," Haze muttered like a cold-blooded killer.

"What is wrong with your husband ma'am?" The female operator questioned.

"I beat him to death with a baseball bat for doing crack," Haze answered not ashamed of nothing that had just taken place.

"I'm sending an ambulance now ma'am and what is your name?" The 911 operator tried to certify.

"Haze Maxine Hilton."

It didn't take long for EMS trucks and police deputies to arrive on the bleeding scene. Paramedics tried to do their medical best to stabilize Chisel, but no matter what they tried he was not stabilizing. Scattered on their condo balconies and front lawns like a pack of nosy crows, everybody was trying to figure out who was about to get arrested and why. Once they saw Chisel being wheeled away in a stretcher into an ambulance, Haze's neighbors weren't stunned at all. They knew it was only a matter of time before that hooker's life was going to come tumbling down like Dominos.

Police arrested Haze on the scene and she didn't detest anything. She was completely anesthetized through all of her indictment procedures. Haze had been in trouble with the law countless times prior to this occasion, only difference was this time her odds wasn't going to be so lucky. It was going to be nearly impossible for Haze to be amended from the consequences of this atrocity. Haze should've thought twice about all of Chisel's family and friends because once they were hip to what she had done to their Chisel, she was going to be apologetic. She was going to want to rededicate her life to the Lord and form a spiritual relationship with him in all forms of her life. She was going to wish that she never laid a bare hand on him and she kept her incriminating hands to herself.

***

Terrace and Angel had been waiting over 30 minutes for their ride to their bus station in the emergency waiting room. Tired of waiting, Terrace asked Angel could he see her phone to check up on their cab, because clearly men were more authoritative then women. As Terrace was re-dialing the Checker Cab Company, an incoming call was coming through. Since Terrace was Angel's man he figured he would answer her phone. The caller id on her phone said Eon and it had a picture of his face to go with it. Irrefutably, Eon was over the whole chainsaw massacre feeling he got at Wiley's house and he wanted to reunite with his friend. Terrace gave Angel a who the fuck is this look and answered.

"Hello," Terrace answered curiously.

"Can I please speak to Angel?" Eon asked kindly not intimidated by a male answering her phone.

"What does Angel need to speak to you for when she has a man?"

"I'm not trying to take your girl or nothing. I just wanted to talk to her about an event that happened over her father's house and make sure she was okay."

"Angel doesn't need you to worry about her well-being. I've got that covered. Whatever you're talking about is in the past. That shit is irrelevant so when you hang up this phone lose her number," Terrace ended.

Angel just sat by Terrace the whole time with the stupid face staring downward knowing that Terrace was about to cuss her out in 1.5 seconds.

"Who the fuck is this peon calling your phone Angel? I can't even go to the hospital without you talking to other niggas behind my back?"

"I wasn't talking to him Terrace please calm down."

"Do you want to make a bet?" Instantly, Terrace began lurking through Angel's phone checking call logs, contacts, and text messages, and his discoveries were right. Angel had been talking too Eon like he was her best friend or something and messaging him vulgar messages and vulgar pictures like she was fucking him. The proof was right there in the pudding. Angel should've pushed CLEAR history and DELETE.

"You a liar Angel are you fucking him? You called him the day I left your house while I was in the hospital. And this text message says that he was outside of your house the same day hours later." After that it wasn't no talking or

227

explaining. Terrace made it up in his mind that he was going to punch Angel's lights out for lying and cheating and as far as he was concerned Mr. Woodward might appreciate that. Since they were at the hospital and Terrace didn't want no witnesses Terrace made Angel get up and walk to the store.

"You know I hate people in my business Angel and you got people turning around staring and shit so let's go to the store somewhere privately," Terrace squoze her arm very aggressively helping her out of her seat.

"So while I was in the hospital you were at your father's house with another nigga cheating on me right?"

"No I wasn't Terrace."

Terrace started directing Angel down an alleyway. He lugged her against a building

228

like she was a garbage can and strapped his hand over her mouth. He took his cigarette lighter out of his pocket and began slowly burning Angel's body part by part starting with her tongue and ending with her feet. Tired of her wrenches and clenches he took his belt off and tied it around her neck and choked her to death until she turned pacific blue. Then he took her body and dumped it in the garbage can that was right next to them. He saw some old newspaper blowing in the back alley that had some shit on their about Wiley Woodward being a corrupt cop and he laughed.

"That bitch actually snitched on her father for me oh well," Terrace thought as he lit the end of the newspaper and threw it in the garbage can with Angel's body. Terrace made sure the whole garbage can was burning

rapidly before he departed from the scene.

"The bitch shouldn't have cheated and

she would still be here today. She could've

been Mrs. Smith, but she didn't want to keep

her legs closed, but now she doesn't have a

choice. I told the bitch I hated liars and

cheaters. Maybe the next bitch will listen," was

Terrace's last affirmations about Angel after

■■■■■■■■■■■■■■■■■■■■■■■■■■■■■■■■■■■■■'

Chapter 16: Comatose

Archenemies and Super Villains

In a comatose state, Chisel was barely alive. Haze literally killed the man for trying to annihilate her reputation with his nonchalant patterns of deceit. His open-headed brain injury, impaired breathing, subdural hemorrhage, lack of wakefulness and awareness was raw. The fact that he was going to need tons of plastic surgery to re-structure his two-faced self back together and the fact that he was never going to be the same if he ever came back to life. Plus the fact that he was at risk at falling into a persistent vegetative state was enough for Haze to sleep at night in her cold, barred chamber.

Mimosa heard about Chisel's beat down and cocaine practices, and gave him the finger. "That's exactly what that sucker gets," Mo thought to herself as she clasped Donnie's arms tighter then a neck clasps a chain.

"Isn't that the guy that you left at the bar that one night," Donnie asked Mo as they were watching and listening to the Fox 2 News cover story of Chisel Simmons.

"It is and I'm glad everything happened exactly the way it happened. If it wasn't for that night I would have never found my way to you," Mo kissed Donnie.

"Sucker his lost, my gain," Donnie declared.

Cyn had heard about Chisel's explosive hospitalization, crack dwellings, and had to get to the Clinton Township Police Department on 37985 Groesbeck herself. Fuck calling crime stoppers, she knew classified information about Haze Hilton so she had to prep herself to play another Emmy role at the police station.

Storming through the Clinton Township PD door's with her ferocity in clear view, Cyn had her radar open for Haze so she could let her have it. Even though, Haze was already in handcuffs that didn't stop Cyn from fusing her anger with her hatred for her as she saw Haze slouching woefully on a booking bench.

"Bitch you did this! Didn't you? Setting his house on fire wasn't enough! Why didn't you just leave him if you felt like you were going to kill the man? Chisel didn't deserve this! I hope they lock your itty bitty ass up for life because you never deserved him!" Cyn screamed as multiple officers tried to tame her.

Haze hadn't seen Cyn in ages, but when she finally realized that one of Chisel's local ass bitches was gracing her presence, she rebutted.

"Would somebody please escort this want to be Kerry Washington ass bitch out of my face before I slid my hands out of these handcuffs and put her ass in a coma too!"

"Bitch you proud because you put your husband in a coma? I want you to come out of those handcuffs so I can beat your ass all the way to the Pacific Ocean and back to Korea!"

"Would somebody please escort Mrs. Hilton to a cell and get this lady out of here, this is not the Jerry Springer show," an officer ordered. Cyn left after the police kicked her out of their threshold. She wished she could've got a little closer to Haze so she could've put her

234

feisty paws on her just one time. She wished

she would've hit the bitch first then presumed

to talk shit at least she would've got a lick in,

but no lick or hit was going to be able to

replace Chisel Simmons if he died without

getting the chance to tell Cyn or their son

goodbye. That was just something that Cyn

was going to have to live with because single

mothers lived with her cold reality every single

day and still managed to maintain. If they could

do it so could Cyn, because it wasn't like

Chisel was daddy of the year anyway.

After doing some soul-searching, Cyn

realized that her and her son needed a fresh

start. A fresh start without Chisel Simmons or

anybody who knew Chisel Simmons. She

realized that she had blindfolded herself by her

odium for a woman who wasn't foreshadowed

by a title, a ring, a marriage license, or an ordinary love. Haze Hilton and Chisel Simmons were meant to be together and Cyn Clarkson didn't have any business interfering in their relationship because no matter what she did or how good she fucked him she was always going to be out of bounds. Cyn's new attitude became "fuck Chisel, I don't even know why I bothered him at this point." Cyn was a fool for love, but her love spell was now broken, and she was on a new rocky road with her son down south somewhere where it never snowed and it hardly ever rained.

***

recognized as the former police chief of the Clinton Township Police Department was indefinitely suspended from all of his police entities while under investigations of internal affairs. Most likely, Wiley was going to be working as a top flight security guard at Rainbow's or something for his misconduct before or after the jail time he was probably going to be serving. Even though Angel was too dead and gone to testify against her father, the fact that he was being accused of such horrific crimes was evidence enough to impinge on his reputation.

Of course when a restaurant crew member was going to take out the trash and saw that the garbage can was blazing he ran and got help. He put the fire out with a nearby hose and after forensics diagnosed the scene, they found traces of a woman's body, and reported that she had been burnt alive. Nydia was hysterical and still Wiley didn't give a shit that they had to bury their first and only child at 15 years-old. Since Angel's body had been discovered, Wiley wasn't even concerned about trying to figure out who did it so he was forbidden to come to Angel's funeral. How could he point any fingers when Angel was fucking everybody anyways? That's what she got for snitching and biting the hand that fed her. And it wasn't like she was doing shit fruitful with her life anyway so mine as well be dead.

***

Haze Hilton's mug shot was priceless so priceless that she smiled like she was a fictional super-villain. American Law was more constitutional then Korean Law so it was no way in hell Haze was going to get a free pass back to Korea, so her Korean law upholders could find her innocent. The death penalty hadn't been carried out in Korea since 1997 so Haze was right where she needed to be to suffer. Charged with Arson, Attempted Murder and Assault with intent to do Great Bodily Harm, Haze was convicted and sentenced to LIFE in prison. Haze pled GUILTY to every single charge that was brought against her shady name with no objections to fight for her freedom. As far as she was concerned nobody was free, nothing was free, and freedom was just a word to manipulate society into believing in equality. "*Dolus eventualis*" is what Haze mumbled to herself everyday which refers to a form of intent where the perpetrator objectively foresees the possibility of his or her act causing death and yet persists regardless of the consequences. Haze was okay with it and was willing to live with her results even though she was about to rot her whole life in prison.

Authorities figured it would be best to remove Chisel Simmons from all of Detroit surroundings until they got vise grips on his two open cases and he either went to Hell or he awoken from his long slumber. In Wetumpka, Alabama research was being done on coma patients and medical experts wanted to use Chisel Simmons as a medical guinea pig in their clinical research. Medical specialists at Elmore Community Hospital claimed to have come up with a medical marvel. They claimed to have revitalized over 100 hospital patients out of their somatic states and Chisel Simmons was going to be next. He was going to be the next survival story streaming live from Elmore Community Hospital.

Multiple tests and analysis's showed that Chisel Simmons was indeed a crack addict, an alcoholic, and had a rough medical history. He did it because of all the euphoric feelings that he felt when he snorted it. He felt an increasing sense of energy and alertness, an extremely elevated mood, and a feeling of supremacy. No woman or being could ever compare to that inner high, and that's just the way it was. Being in a coma was exactly what he needed at this ratchet place in his life where he needed some detoxification and to re-evaluate his life.

Chisel was giving doctors a run for their money because no matter what they tried, he wouldn't budge out of his coma. Eventually, if doctors didn't make any progress with him they were going to have to reach out to his family members back in Michigan and let whoever come forward and make the ultimate decision. Let him live or take him off of life support. Let him live or take him off of life support. And if nobody came forward doctors were going to reach out to Cyn Clarkson since they heard through the grapevine that Chisel had 2 known baby mothers one behind bars and one who deserted Michigan. Doctors were just going to have to wait to see what happened, but there was nothing wrong with hypothetically thinking. Chisel Simmons and his liquid atrocities finally got the best of him, and maybe he was wrong and right at the same damn time. Maybe death was the only thing that could stop him from his neurotic addictions, or maybe his addictions were never products of life, they were all just mirages in his thick little head the whole time.

The End

"Liquid Love"

A poem inspired from a real relationship

The liquid hideaway

Stupefied by a swallow

Trapped in the nebula of a bottle

Faithfully unloved

I push and tug at his sobriety

But his consistency never survives

That alcoholic thrive, catastrophic tideway

*Always recaptures him after my moonlight
kisses*

rapture him

He still feels voided

Riven vows of quitting

Complementary forgiveness given,

Forgave, forgiven

The liquid is forbidden

But his disloyalty lingers on

As if his heart doesn't recollect where home is

His selfishness is cloudy cloud

Rowed up by his unlocked insecurities

Life instigates every time

Anger and liquor, liquor and doubt

He's a liquid communicator

Rather drink then talk

Solve the pulse

That comes after the false convictions

The redemption is like a temp-to-hire

Apologetic, unapologetic

Steady harping on old truths

To keep reviving and relying

On his liquid obsession

He's killing his woman softly

And doesn't even know it

Pretends like he doesn't know it

But his knowledge is competent

Her involuntary tears show it

But her tears are never counted

Despite all the disputes that they've been

Mounted on her cheeks

He never sees her cry

Because he's never his true self

He swore he would never ever hurt her

He claimed to love her so indefinitely

So why is she always brawling

With this alcoholic character he created

To mend what, contend what?

He wants to be the biggest loser

Drunken-user, non-stop usages

Let it go or let her go

To have an ordinary love

She deserved so much good love

Because liquid love ain't good

I need a hood over my heart

It's to damaged to manage

I got to banish it

I want real love cuz liquid love ain't it

I want real love your liquid love ain't shit...